ONCE a MARINE

CAT GRANT

FOR
WALT—

GREAT TO
MEET YOU
@ GRL 2012—
XOXO,
Cat Grant

RIPTIDE
PUBLISHING

Riptide Publishing
PO Box 6652
Hillsborough, NJ 08844
http://www.riptidepublishing.com

Cover Art by Reese Dante, www.reesedante.com
Layout: L.C. Chase, lcchase.com/design.htm
Editors: Aleksandr Voinov and Rachel Haimowitz

ISBN: 978-1-937551-24-7

Printed in the United States of America
First edition
January, 2012

Also available in ebook
Ebook ISBN: 978-1-937551-11-7

For Aleks and Rachel—thanks for having faith in me!

Chapter 1

November, 2009

The second he walked into the diner, I nearly dropped the stack of plates I was carrying. Six foot three at least, with long, long legs encased in jeans worn almost white across the front of his well-muscled thighs. Dripping wet from the freezing November downpour, he unzipped his rain jacket and pushed back the hood. *Oh, holy Christ.* Lush lips, strong chin, cheekbones that could slice through a rare steak. Nordic-god blond hair in a military buzz cut that instantly made the crotch of my jeans tight. Good thing I had my apron on. I pushed my glasses up the bridge of my nose and kept staring.

I wasn't the only one. Terry's hand froze momentarily over the cash register as our new arrival gave her a quick nod, grabbed the sports section from the front counter, and headed for the nearest empty table. He didn't seem to notice us both gaping at him, or maybe he just didn't care. Drop-dead gorgeous guys like him were probably used to it.

"That's what I call a tall, cool drink of water." Terry handed her customer his change and shut the register with a bump of her ample hip. "And lucky you—he just sat down in your section. Unless you want to take your break now?" She flashed me a toothy grin.

"Nice try," I fired back with a wink. I put my armload of dirty dishes in a tub under the counter and grabbed a mug and a pot of coffee before making a beeline back to Mr. Tall-and-Hunky's table. The shitty weather had scared away most of the usual Sunday morning crowd, so for once I didn't get waylaid refilling cups.

Tall-and-Hunky glanced up as I approached. He looked about thirty, with nice eyes—pale blue, but not the least bit icy. Smiling, I gestured toward him with the mug. "Hi, I'm Marc. Would you like some coffee?" He nodded. "Did you want some juice this morning as well, or maybe some water?"

"Coffee's fine, thanks." For a second I could've sworn I detected the soft lilt of a southern accent. And now I definitely recognized the haircut—shaved nearly bare on the back and sides, flat on top. The traditional "high and tight" cut worn by most Marines. Sweet, seedy memories of falling to my knees in the back room of an adult bookstore in Oceanside raced through my brain as I watched him stir raw sugar into his coffee and take his first tentative sip.

Then those big blue eyes locked on mine, jolting me back to the present. "Um, do you need a couple more minutes to make up your mind?"

He snagged a menu and gave it a quick once-over, the side with "Blue Windmill Café" printed on it flipped toward me. "I'll have two eggs over easy with hash browns and a side of bacon."

There it was, and no doubt this time—that unmistakable slow-as-honey Carolina drawl. Just like Rob, I realized with a pang, tugging my pad and pen from my apron to scribble down his order. "What kind of toast?"

"You got biscuits?" he asked shyly, one corner of his mouth quirking up.

"Afraid not. How about an English muffin?"

"That'll do. Thanks." He took another sip of his coffee and turned his attention back to the sports section.

"Looked like you were having a nice conversation," Terry commented archly as I came back around the counter and stuck my order in the queue for Fernando. The smell of burnt toast and bacon grease floated forth from the kitchen, punctuated by the clatter of Fernando's teenage son Pedro none-too-gently loading dirty dishes into the washer. "Did you notice him checking out your butt?"

"Yeah, right." Six months ago, she might've had me going. Terry loved yanking my chain. Good-natured yanking, but still.

"For once I'm not kidding. He looked right at those cute little buns of yours when you turned around."

I tossed a nonchalant glance in Military Guy's direction. He had his phone out now, and was punching at its tiny keyboard with mad double-thumb action. It looked like a toy nestled in his huge, long-fingered hands. *Oh, dear God.* If there was one thing I went crazy for, it was a guy with nice hands.

"Just my luck." Terry shook her head, brunette ponytail swinging to and fro. "All the hot ones play for your team."

"I think the jury's still out on that."

"Why don't we put it to the test?" She snapped up a coffee pot from a burner. "Let's see if he needs a warm-up."

Of course, crotchety old Mr. Faber had to choose that moment to hobble up to the register to pay his bill. I rang him up while trying to peer over his shoulder to see what Terry was doing.

She could flirt with the best of them, I'd give her that. Hand resting seductively on her cocked hip, she gave Military Guy a big smile and batted her lashes. He smiled back, his gaze lingering on her impressive bust line. Didn't mean anything one way or the other—hell, I stared at Terry's tits too, mostly because they seemed to defy gravity. They exchanged words, but I couldn't hear what either of them said. Finally, she topped off his mug and sashayed back to the counter.

"His mama raised him right," she announced with a rapturous sigh. "Such lovely manners. He actually called me ma'am!"

I snickered. "Probably because you remind him of his mom."

"Watch it, buster. I'm only thirty-five."

According to Fernando, Terry'd just celebrated the sixth anniversary of her thirty-fifth birthday. But since I didn't want to get kicked in the shin, I figured I'd better not mention it. Besides, my order was up.

I stacked both plates along my left arm like a seasoned greasy-spoon pro, grabbed a bottle of ketchup, and motored back to Military Guy's table. He folded his paper and sat back, giving me room to set everything down. The plate with the bacon and eggs nearly slipped from my hand when he shrugged out of his slicker. He was wearing a plain black t-shirt underneath. A really *tight* plain black t-shirt stretched over every hard, smooth muscle in his chest and shoulders, showing off a spectacular set of guns. It was all I could do to keep from drooling.

"A-anything else I can get you?" Coffee? Tea? *Me*?

"This'll do for now, thanks." His right sleeve hiked up when he reached for his fork, revealing a small tattoo of a bulldog with "USMC" emblazoned under it. Growing up in San Diego, I'd seen my fair share of Marine Corps tats. Most of them looked garish and trashy, but this one was actually kind of cute. So was this guy a real Marine, or just a wannabe?

One way to find out. "We don't get too many devil dogs in this neighborhood. You here to protect Berkeley from the scourge of all us bleeding-heart liberals?"

His smile immediately faded. "I think I'm a little late for that. Besides, I'm not on active duty."

Ouch. Now I wished I'd kept my mouth shut. "Well, let me know if you need anything else, okay?"

"Will do."

Before long, the rain slowed to a trickle and business started to pick up. Within half an hour, the place was packed, and Terry and I were running our butts off. Pedro even had to come out front to help bus tables and ring up customers. I got so busy I didn't notice when Military Guy got up to leave. The next time I looked over at his table, he was gone.

Royally bummed, I went to clear off his dirty dishes—and there was his phone, under the discarded sports section he'd been reading. It was one of those pocket-sized prepaid models. People left them here all the time. They were so cheap he'd probably rather buy another one than retrace his steps to find it. Oh well. I'd toss it in the lost and found anyway.

He'd left a generous tip: five bucks on a breakfast that cost less than ten. A kind gesture, especially since I'd forgotten to come back and check on him. Not only damn cute, but a gentleman to boot—and with my luck, probably straight as a steel ruler. Best to put him out of my mind right now. I shoved the phone in my pocket, added his dirty plates to my ever-growing stack, and toted it all back to the front counter.

The sun started poking through the remaining cloud cover by the time I got off shift at three. I headed down the block toward the bus stop, zipping up my jacket against the lingering chill. Typical Bay Area weather—cold, wet, and gloomy from now until March. The air tasted good, though, scrubbed fresh and clean by the rain.

Bus service ran slow on Sundays, so I ducked inside the shelter to wait, burying my hands in my jeans pockets. My fingers closed over something small and plastic. *Shit*, the Marine's phone! A twinge of guilt plucked at me as I yanked it from my pocket and flicked it on. What was the harm in finding out his name? It wasn't like I was planning to stalk him. One quick look, then I'd put the damn thing in the lost and found tomorrow.

Cole Hammond. A good, strong name with a touch of country twang. It suited him. His address was right below. It was only about three blocks north. Huh. Wonder why I'd never seen him in the diner before today?

Ten minutes crawled by, and still no sign of the bus. Fuck it—I might as well walk. Except my apartment lay south while my legs insisted on carrying me in the opposite direction, toward Cole Hammond's place.

It was your usual depressing gray concrete apartment building on Channing, within easy walking distance of the UC Berkeley campus. I'd lived in one of the residence halls not far from here during my undergrad days. So was this Cole guy a student? He looked a little old to be getting his bachelor's, but grad school was a possibility. Maybe he was studying for an advanced science or engineering degree on the government's dime. He certainly seemed better-spoken than the average grunt. Of course, if Uncle Sam was forking out the money to send him here, he was probably an officer.

I found his name on the complex's directory, then started to waver big-time. This was nuts. What the fuck was I thinking? I should just drop the phone in his mailbox and get out of here before one of the other residents saw me loitering and called the cops. Except it wouldn't fit in the mailbox—the slats weren't wide enough. And if I left it on the table in the foyer, it'd end up getting stolen.

I could bring it up to his apartment. Leave it outside his door, knock, then take off before anybody saw me. Like leaving a bag of burning dog shit on someone's stoop at Halloween, only slightly more considerate. Might as well do it and get it over with. I'd already come this far.

His apartment was on the third floor. I decided to take the stairs instead of the elevator. The place was a labyrinth of hallways, but finally I found the right one. As I rounded the corner, I saw someone else approaching from the other end of the corridor.

Oh, God, it was him!

He was carrying a Whole Foods bag in one arm, a six-pack of beer tucked under the other. Fat Tire, from the look of it. Funny, but I would've pegged him as a Bud or Michelob man. Those big blue eyes of his widened the moment he recognized me, and he stopped dead right in the middle of the hallway.

I held up his phone and forced a shaky smile. Didn't want him thinking I'd shown up to mug him, though the mere idea of that was pretty fucking hilarious. He could probably flatten me with a flick of his pinkie. "You forgot something."

"Holy shit." Shoulders relaxing, he set down his groceries and started checking his pockets. Guess he just wanted to make sure. "I didn't even know it was missing. Thanks, man. I appreciate you goin' out of your way."

The drawl was back, even stronger this time. "It was the least I could do after that nice tip you left me."

"No problem. I waited tables every summer during high school. It's a tough job." He jerked his chin toward his apartment. "I was gonna crack open a cold one and watch the game. Wanna join me?"

Nothing like Southern hospitality. I smiled and said, "Sure, why not?" then followed him inside.

It was a one-bedroom unit overlooking a tiny green patch of courtyard and another apartment building across the way. Cramped living room just big enough for a couch, a coffee table, and a small flat-screen TV. Galley-style kitchen. A short hallway on the right-hand side of the living room led—presumably—to the bedroom and bathroom.

The place looked like an army of maids had just swept through, except for a laptop computer sitting open on the coffee table, surrounded by several books and piles of papers. One thick volume had "Contract Law" stamped on its spine in bold silver type.

"Law school, huh? You enrolled at Boalt Hall?"

He looked up from putting his groceries away and nodded.

"Yup. Just started this term."

"How do you like it?"

"It's okay. A lot harder than I expected, though." He snagged a couple bottles, twisted them open and brought them over. At his nod, we both sat down, the couch springs creaking under our weight. A little lumpy, but not too uncomfortable for something he'd probably bought at a thrift store. Scooping up the remote, he flicked on the TV. It was on a commercial, so he muted the sound.

"So you've been in town since, what?" I asked. "Last August? And today's the first time you dropped by the diner?"

"I meant to stop in before. I pass the place every day when I'm out running. I don't have a whole lot of money to spend on restaurants, but today I decided to treat myself and celebrate a belated birthday."

"Well, happy birthday!" I leaned over to clink bottles, but he put up a hand to stop me. "You don't want to drink to it?"

"It's not mine. It's the USMC's. Or it was, last week. November 10th."

Oh, yeah. Rob and all his buddies used to make such a big deal out of it, going around slapping each other on the back and wishing each other happy birthday as if every damn Marine on the planet had been born on the same day.

"You're not on active duty anymore, but you still celebrate?"

"Just upholding tradition," he replied with a shrug, then flicked the TV's sound back on.

Football wasn't my favorite sport. I didn't even recognize which teams were playing. After a few minutes, my attention started to wander. I glanced around the room, struck by the starkness of its bare white walls. No diplomas, no citations, no photographs. No reminders of home or family. Seemed a bit odd.

We'd finished our beers by the time the next commercial came on, so he got up to get us a second round.

"Don't you get bored with nothing to look at except that little garden outside your window?" I asked.

He chuckled. "I don't have time to get bored. School keeps me hoppin'. 'Sides, I'd rather look at four empty walls than miles and miles of fuckin' sand."

"You were in Iraq?"

"Yup. Five tours." Mouth tightening, he handed me a fresh bottle and sat back down.

Holy shit. I should've dropped the subject, but curiosity got the better of me. "In Baghdad?"

"And Fallujah. Both times."

For a long moment, all I could do was stare. This guy had survived two of the ugliest and most brutal battles of the entire war. Despite my left-leaning politics, I couldn't help but admire him. "Looks like you made it through in one piece."

"Relatively speaking." Up went that cute little quirk of his lips again, then he turned his attention back to the game.

We downed our beer more quickly this time. By the time I reached the bottom of my bottle, I had a sweet buzz going. Cole got back up at the next commercial to fetch us another round. I was about to tell him I'd had enough, but his blue gaze locked on mine as he handed it to me, and the words dried up in my throat.

This time he sat down closer to me—close enough to touch—slumping down and stretching his arm along the back of the couch. I went stiff for a second or two, but then leaned my head back until it rested against his forearm. His toned, well-muscled forearm, dusted with soft, pale hair that felt like silk against the nape of my neck. He glanced over, giving me a quick smile.

What the *fuck?* Was he sending me signals, or just trying to hang out and relax? He already had my heart racing, but still, I didn't want to presume. If not for the good sense to know when to turn tail and run, I'd have gotten my lights punched out more than once making moves on guys who claimed to be straight. But Cole hadn't claimed anything; I'd simply made an assumption. A possibly erroneous assumption. Even so, was it worth the risk to find out?

Another long sip of beer, and my left hand made the decision for me. My breath froze in my lungs as I cupped Cole's knee and gave it a gentle squeeze. I shut my eyes, half-expecting him to haul off and slug me, or at least push me away, but instead I felt his calloused fingers stroke my cheek, the pad of his thumb worry at my lower lip.

"You got a pretty mouth," he whispered, beer and arousal lowering his tone to a raspy growl. "Why don't you use it?"

No way to misinterpret that. I set my beer down, dropped to my knees between his splayed legs and looked up at him, making sure he really meant it. The hot glow in his eyes and the way his breath quickened, the tip of his tongue darting out to wet his lips, told me all I needed to know.

His cock stood straight up under his fly, a hard ridge practically bursting through the zipper. I eased it down gently, surprised to discover blue and white checkered boxers underneath. Every other Marine I'd been with had either worn briefs or tighty-whities. Time spun back, and I could practically feel the sticky floor of a video booth beneath my knees, that first grunt's big, sweaty paw gripping my neck as he shoved his dick down my throat. Dizzy from the memory and the scent of Cole's pre-cum, I let my eyes drift closed and leaned forward to suck the tip of his cock between my lips.

God, he tasted good. Salty and bitter, a perfect, luscious mouthful. Almost too big for me to handle, which I should've expected—guys his height were usually hung like mules. So I opened wide, sliding down until he hit the back of my throat, then relaxed, breathed deep through my nose, and swallowed.

Cole gasped, digging his hands into the cushions, gave a couple of jerky thrusts and came.

I kept sucking him until he finished, not wanting to miss a single drop. At last I pulled off gently, tucked him back into his boxers and zipped him up. "Short and sweet," I said with a smile, wiping the corners of my mouth, "but I guess I should take it as a compliment, huh?"

"Um, yeah." He sat up straight, face bright pink, raking a hand through his hair. His fingers trembled as he scooped up the remote and turned off the TV, even though the game wasn't over yet. "I've got some studying to do, so . . ."

I gaped at him, wondering if I needed to clean the wax out of my ears. "So you're kicking me out?"

"Look, time just got away from me. I got a shitload of reading I need to catch up on—"

His lips kept moving, but I stopped listening. I'd heard this song before. Now that he'd gotten off, he wanted me gone. I hadn't thought he was that kind of a guy, but of course he was. They all were. Even after the hell Rob and Tony had put me through, here I was, falling for a hot haircut and a nice set of muscles all over again. How could I be such a fucking idiot?

"Yeah, right," I snapped, finally cutting him off. "Don't worry, I get it. I'm going." I got up, grabbed my jacket, and practically sprinted for the door, half-hoping Cole would come after me.

He didn't.

I'd no sooner stepped from the building's foyer when it started raining again. I yanked up the hood of my jacket, shoved my hands in my pockets, and headed south, toward my place. Maybe a long walk would help me cool off and feel slightly less cheap and humiliated, but somehow I doubted it.

Terry was standing outside the kitchen door puffing on a Marlboro Light and casting a glare at the overcast sky when I arrived for the lunch shift on Monday. "Isn't it a little early for your break?" I asked, ducking past her to hang my jacket on the peg next to the time clock.

"Pedro's out front. He can handle it by himself for a few minutes. It's been dead pretty much all morning." She took her last drag, dropped the butt on the ground and stamped it out with the heel of her sneaker. "That hottie dropped by again. He seemed kind of bummed when I told him you weren't here yet. Asked me to give you this." She fished in her apron pocket, pulling out a folded square of yellow scratch paper, the kind we used for scribbling down to-go orders. "Don't worry, I didn't read it," she added with a crooked grin.

I didn't want to read it either. In fact, I was tempted to pitch it in the trash, but instead I turned around and slowly opened the note. "Sorry about yesterday," it read. "I didn't mean to upset you. Regards, Cole." Not exactly the warmest apology ever, but at least he hadn't insulted me with the old, "Wow, was I drunk!" excuse. Not that it mattered a damn. If he showed his face here again, I'd let Terry wait on him.

God, it was chilly standing in the doorway. I didn't realize I'd started to shiver until Terry's hand slid onto my shoulder. "Did something happen, sweetie? You can tell me."

"It's nothing," I mumbled, "He, um, left his phone on the table yesterday, so I decided to return it to him, and . . ." And that was it. The rest of the story poured out of me before I could stop it.

"So you blew him, then he blew you off?" She rolled her eyes. "Jerk. If it's any consolation, I've had a couple exes just like him."

"Me too. Which means I should've known better."

"Men! Can't live with 'em—and if you shoot 'em, you have to find a place to bury the bodies. Too much goddamn trouble either way." Smiling, she gave me a quick hug. "Don't beat yourself up about it, hon. It's his loss."

I worked 'til seven, then asked Fernando to make me a chicken salad sandwich to take home. Most of the time I made an effort to cook, even if it was only scrambled eggs and toast, but tonight I wanted to get in a couple hours of writing time before bed. I needed to finish my latest chapter and email it to my critique partner so he could read it over before our meeting tomorrow. Guilt pricked at me for squeezing it in under the wire, but lately I'd been having trouble staying motivated. Meeting with Ben every other week gave me a much-needed kick in the ass.

As I trudged up the steps to my apartment, I spied my cat sitting in the window. He scampered over to greet me the moment I got the door open, blinking his lime-green eyes as he meowed and tried to claw his way up my leg. A quick glance at his empty bowl in the far corner of the kitchen told me why. I put my sandwich in the fridge, then dug the Friskies bag out from under the kitchen sink and gave him a generous handful. "Here you go, Thomas," I said, getting in one scritch before he nudged me aside, buried his black-and-white face in kibbly nirvana, and started crunching.

"So much for feline affection," I muttered. "If you had opposable thumbs, you wouldn't need me at all, would you?"

Thomas munched on, not paying me the slightest bit of attention.

With a resigned sigh, I put the cat food away and ambled into my living room-slash-bedroom. A double bed, a desk, a chair, a table, a ratty Turkish throw rug I hadn't bothered vacuuming in a while. Shelves filled with used books, DVDs, and CDs lined the entire left-hand wall. A writer needed his muses, after all, and mine were stories and music. I had a TV too, a decrepit thing I hadn't bothered turning on in ages. I couldn't afford cable, so I usually just watched DVDs on my laptop.

Five years in the same place, and damn if it didn't look it. Could've used a fresh coat of paint to brighten things up, but what was the point? I hardly ever had anybody over. The last guy I'd dated had stopped calling months ago, and after what'd happened with Cole the other day . . . Jesus, what the fuck was my problem? Why did I only attract guys who decided I wasn't worth the trouble?

I kicked off my sneakers and stretched, trying to work the ache out of my legs and lower back. Most of the time it didn't bother me too much; I'd gotten used to spending eight hours or more on my feet. I hadn't always waited tables, but even when I taught at Berkeley City College, I stood for hours every day in the lecture hall. Then the shitty economy took its toll, and budget cuts eliminated my position. Sure, I could've tried for a nice boring office job, but all the decent-paying ones were across the bridge in the city, and no way was I about to tackle that nightmare commute every day. Besides, the thought of putting on a suit and tie made me shudder.

Weirdly enough, the diner had proved a good fit. Minimum wage, but most days I raked in decent tips, and it sure as hell kept me more active than sitting behind a desk. Even so, this wasn't where I'd envisioned myself five years ago. Almost thirty, with a master's degree under my belt, and here I was slinging hash to pay my rent when what I really wanted to do was write all day.

But for now, I'd have to be content with writing all evening. Dropping into my desk chair, I rolled my stiff neck, opened my laptop, and fired it up. Checked email, deleted spam, skimmed the dozen or so remaining messages for a glimmer of possible importance. And oh my God, there it was, the one that'd had me on pins and needles for the past month: a contract offer on my latest book. I finished reading the email, then scrolled back to the beginning and read it again, dancing on my chair.

My ninth sale in the past three years, and every time was a genuine thrill. Best of all, each new book made more money than the last. No, I wasn't raking in big-time bucks yet, but with the way my sales were increasing, I might be able to quit my day job in the next couple of years.

I considered grabbing a celebratory beer from the fridge, but it just reminded me of yesterday with Cole. No time to dwell on that now. I cued up my favorite Mahler symphony instead, opened my current manuscript, and got to work.

Chapter 2

Cole jerked awake with a soft cry, heart pounding, screams and explosions echoing in his skull. Took a few moments before the warm blanket over him and the pale gray light from the streetlamp outside his window reminded him where he was.

Groping blindly, he found the vial of Xanax on his bedside table and swallowed one dry, then shut his eyes and tried to concentrate on slowing his breathing. Finally his pulse stopped racing and he sat up, squinting at the clock radio. Closing in on oh-four-thirty. No point trying to go back to sleep when he had to be up in half an hour anyway. He switched off the alarm and padded into the bathroom to splash cold water on his face. Then, marginally more awake, he threw his robe on over his boxers and headed for the kitchen to make coffee.

His first class was at eight, but he tried to put in an hour or two of caffeine-fueled refresher study before he went out on his run. He had to, if only to keep up with his classmates. Jesus, he was getting old—or maybe he'd just been out of school too long. He didn't have to report for formation every day like he had back at the Academy, and there was no compulsory PT. All he had to do was study his ass off, and he could barely manage that. He was lagging at least a chapter behind in every fucking class.

He washed up the stack of dishes in the sink while he waited for his coffee to brew, and had just finished putting everything away when his gaze landed on the cordless phone at the far end of the kitchen counter, its message light blinking urgently. It had to be his mother. She was the only one who ever called him on the landline.

The coffeemaker dinged. Cole poured himself a tall mug and took a sip, reveling in that first glorious taste of morning joe. Then he grabbed the phone and went to sit down on the couch. It was almost eight o'clock back home; his parents were sure to be up. Maybe he'd get lucky and his mother would answer. If not, well, he could always hang up.

He hit the speed-dial and held his breath. The line clicked on after the second ring. "Hello?" came a woman's soft voice.

"Hey, Mama. Sorry I didn't call you back yesterday. I got kind of busy this weekend with studying and all." Not the whole truth, but he couldn't exactly tell her what he'd been doing yesterday afternoon, or with whom. He stared at the empty cushion beside him, his gut tightening. "How's everything at home?"

"Oh, we had a bit of a gully-washer this week, what with Hurricane Ida and that nor'easter blowing down the coast. Your father's still trying to adjust to retirement. Talk about a bull in a china shop!" She laughed. "He's up with the chickens every day, out in the garage working on restoring that old Mustang."

Dad had been tinkering with that heap of junk for years now. They'd worked on it together during his brief summer and holiday visits when he'd been at the Academy. It pained him to think he'd probably never get to help his father with it again. "Glad to hear it," he murmured.

He waited for her to continue, but the silence stretched out a bit too long for comfort. "Everything okay, Mama?"

"Oh, don't mind me. Just lost my train of thought for a minute." She laughed nervously, paused again. "The real reason I called was to find out your plans for Thanksgiving. It's only a couple weeks away."

Jesus. He hadn't even thought about Thanksgiving. Or

Christmas. Or anything except getting through the term without flunking out. "Honestly, Mama," he began as gently as he could, "I don't think I can make it this year. I'm sorry."

"Well, I'll admit I'm disappointed. The whole family's going to miss you."

He chuckled bitterly. "I doubt that."

"Cole, you need to give him time. He'll come around. He always does."

His hand tensed on the phone. "You weren't there, Mama. You didn't hear the things he said. That I was a disgrace to the Corps. That the sight of me turned his stomach. That he was ashamed to call me his son."

"Oh, Cole . . ." Her voice wavered. Cole prayed to God it wouldn't crack, or he might crack too. "He's trying, he really is. We both are. This isn't an easy thing to come to terms with."

That earned her a short, ugly bark of laughter.

"Sweetheart, listen to me—"

"No, you listen to me." Stunned silence crackled on the other end of the line. He'd never interrupted her before. Never spoken to her in such an angry tone. But there was no other way to make her understand. "I can't help who I am. I've been struggling with it for years, and maybe one of these days I'll finally get right with it. As far as the Corps goes, telling them the truth about me was the only honorable thing to do. The only thing I *could* do. I'm sorry if Dad can't accept that. But I'm not about to fly three thousand miles to sit across the dinner table from someone who's ashamed of me."

"I wish there was something I could say to change your mind. I wish I could snap my fingers and put things back the way they used to be."

Well, of course that's what she wanted. Sweep all the unpleasant shit under the rug and pretend it'd never happened. It was the Hammond family way. "I should get back to studying."

Another sigh. "All right. Take care of yourself. I know you're busy, but I worry."

"I'll be fine. Talk to you again soon." He clicked off the phone and tossed it on the table, then slumped back on the couch. God, he was such a fucking hypocrite. All his talk about honor, yet he still didn't have the courage to act on it. To be who he was, honestly and openly. Thirty years old, and still picking up guys on the sly for quick fucks and furtive blowjobs. Just like that guy yesterday—what was his name? Marc? He'd seemed nice enough. Easy to talk to. He didn't deserve to get tossed aside like a used rubber thirty seconds after Cole had come in his mouth.

And here came the anxiety again, slightly dulled by the Xanax he'd swallowed earlier. He'd taken it so often lately, he probably needed to start upping the dosage. Well, fuck that. He wasn't about to let himself become dependent on pills. He chugged down the rest of his lukewarm coffee and rolled to his feet. Maybe a run would make him feel better. It sure as hell couldn't make him feel worse.

Chapter 3

I arrived a few minutes late for my meeting with Ben. The campus coffeehouse was bustling with students dashing in for a between-class caffeine fix, but luckily, Ben had already snagged a table next to the big picture window overlooking the quad. A steaming cup sat in front of the single empty chair. I sank down, shrugged out of my damp rain slicker, and took a grateful sip. My favorite ginger peach green tea. God, Ben was such a considerate sweetie. I didn't realize he'd paid attention to what I usually ordered.

"Thanks," I said, digging in my backpack for a few bucks to cover it. "Sorry to keep you waiting. The bus ran late."

"No problem" was all I caught before the rumble of a couple dozen other voices drowned him out. I leaned across the table to hear better as he opened his messenger bag and pulled out some pages. "I made a few notes on your chapter," he said, "although I don't know how useful they'll be." He shrugged. "You're a lot better at this critiquing stuff than I am. Honestly, I sort of feel like I'm wasting your time."

"Don't sell yourself short. You've got good instincts. I wouldn't bother working with you otherwise."

Ben took a sip of his latte while I flipped through my chapter, skimming the comments scribbled in red pen. I'd told him I wrote gay romance before we decided to start meeting, but this was the first chapter I'd given him with actual sex in it. The sex scene, however, had no comments on it at all. A twinge of apprehension rippled through me. "Didn't you read the whole thing?"

"Yeah, of course. I just didn't know what to say about the last part. I mean, it's well written and all, but . . ."

"Not really your thing?" I supplied with a lopsided smile. "S'okay, I get it."

Ben nodded. "It's just a little outside my comfort zone. But you keep saying I need to push past it, so I'll try harder next time." He flicked the handle of his mug with his thumb, smiling nervously. "Actually, my girlfriend picked up the last few pages and started reading it. She said it was pretty hot."

I laughed, relieved. "Nothing like appealing to your target audience, huh?"

We went over the rest of his comments, then moved on to discussing Ben's latest chapter. His style was more literary than mine, with some absolutely gorgeous, lyrical prose I couldn't help but envy. Unfortunately, his pacing dragged like a broken ankle.

We discussed how to fix it, then I downed my last sip of cold tea and stole a glance at my watch. Closing in on three o'clock. I needed to get home and start turning out some new pages. "Why don't we meet at my place next time? That way we won't have to shout across the table."

"Okay by me."

We got up together, and exchanged hugs before heading out. The rain had stopped, but the air was still brisk enough to make me zip my jacket. I crossed the street at Bancroft and plodded down Telegraph toward my bus stop. Maybe eleven years of living here had left me jaded. The head shops and panhandlers barely registered, though the familiar bouquet of takeout pizza, garbage, and urine still made my nostrils twitch. Then I heard a telltale slap of sneakers on damp pavement and swung around, figuring Ben had decided to come after me.

Only it wasn't Ben. It was Cole Hammond, looking positively *edible* in those worn jeans and a navy blue hoodie.

Twin spots of color popped high and bright on those amazing cheekbones as I met his eyes.

"What do you want?" I snapped.

His expression crumpled. What, did he think I'd be overjoyed to see him? "I, um, I saw you through the window at the coffeehouse."

"So you're stalking me now? After the shit you pulled the other day? You can't make up your mind, can you?"

"I wanted to see if you got my note."

I couldn't *believe* this guy. He'd chased me all the way down the street just to make absolutely, positively sure I knew he'd blown me off? "Yeah, I got it. Message received loud and clear—*get lost*."

"That's not what I meant."

"Really? Because you seemed pretty fucking adamant about it on Sunday."

"Look, I'm sorry about that. I was an asshole."

I blinked. Wow. A Marine actually admitting he was wrong. Was this opposite day? "Yeah, you were. Which is too bad, because I thought we were having a good time."

"Me too." Now there was a nice smile—shy, warm, and sincere, with a tiny flash of white. "Is there any way I can make it up to you?"

If he'd asked me yesterday, or even this morning, I would've laughed in his face. So why wasn't I doing it now? A smile and a little groveling—was that really all it took to rinse away Sunday's bitter aftertaste? "Fine. You've just earned yourself a chance to take me out for coffee. Let's go."

Cole shook his head. "I've got class in about fifteen minutes. How about tomorrow night?"

I made a show of pondering it for a few seconds before nodding. Didn't want him to think I was a *total* pushover. "I get off work at seven. Drop by the diner and pick me up. But fair warning: if you stand me up, there won't be a next time."

His smile widened and my knees turned to jelly. Damn it, how the hell was I supposed to stay mad at him when he looked so damn sincere and adorable? "Looking forward to it."

I watched him walk away, mesmerized by the sight of his ass in those tight jeans. Even after the other day, he still got to me on the most primal level. Oh God, not good. Not good at *all.*

CHAPTER 4

"You're antsy tonight." Terry looked up from refilling the salt shakers, her sharp gaze following mine up to the clock over the kitchen door. Five minutes 'til seven, and still no sign of Cole. "What's the matter, you got a hot date or something?"

I shrugged. "Maybe. Maybe not."

"What's that supposed to mean?"

"Nothing." Four minutes 'til seven. I might as well face it—he wasn't coming. Stifling a pissed-off sigh, I grabbed a towel and wiped down the front counter. Just as I turned around to start cleaning the milkshake blender, the bell over the door dinged. And there stood Cole in black jeans, that tight black t-shirt, and a black leather jacket that clung to his shoulders and biceps like a second skin.

Jesus.

I cast a pointed glance at the clock. Two minutes after the hour. "You're late," I said, barely stifling a grin.

"Really?" He pushed back his left sleeve to show me his watch. "Mine says seven on the dot."

"Okay. You get a pass—this time."

He grinned. "I thought I might."

I was about to tell him not to get cocky—for all the good it'd do—until Terry shot me a look that could flay skin at fifty paces and jerked her chin toward the kitchen. "Have a seat," I told Cole. "I should be done here in a few minutes."

The kitchen door had barely swung shut before she lit into me. "Just what the hell do you think you're doing? Three days ago that guy had you practically in tears!"

"I know. But he apologized, and he meant it. I decided to give him another chance."

"Another chance to break your heart? Great idea."

"Terry, c'mon. No need to get all overprotective. I'm a big boy."

I tried to scoot past her, but she planted her hands on her hips and refused to budge. "You both are. That's what worries me."

"It's just coffee and conversation. Nothing else is gonna happen."

"Does *he* know that?"

I smiled and threw my arms around her. "You're sweet for being so concerned, but butt out, okay?"

"Fine." She pushed me away and jabbed a finger at my chest. "But don't come crying to me when he skips out and leaves you sleeping on the wet spot. What is it with you and jarheads anyway? One look, and every last scrap of sense flies right out of your brain."

"He's not your average jarhead," I said, taking off my apron. "Sorry Terry, gotta go."

When I emerged from the kitchen, Cole slid off his stool. "Ready to go?" I asked. He nodded and stepped toward the door, holding it open for me. No one had done that for me in ages. Not since Rob, in fact. Took me aback for a second or two, but then I smiled and led the way.

It seemed like a pleasant evening, the sky a deep blue with a few scattered clouds. Cole and I took a leisurely stroll to Peet's a couple blocks down. I'd intended to pay for my own tea, but he whipped out his debit card first, shaking his head when I tried to push a few bucks into his hand.

"I'm not so poor that I can't afford to buy my date a drink," he said as we found a quiet corner table and sat down.

"Who said this was a date?"

"Two people making an appointment to socialize? What else would you call it?"

He had a point. Nodding, I slipped off my jacket. Just sitting across the table from him made me feel warm enough. "Something tells me you haven't been on a lot of dates lately."

"If you're talking about what we did the other day, it's been a few months. If you're talking about what we're doing now . . ." He shook his head. "To be honest, I don't even remember. At least five years."

God, no wonder he'd been so eager to let me blow him. "You been in the Corps a long time?"

"Since I was eighteen."

"Annapolis?"

His eyes widened. "How'd you know?"

"You don't act like any of the grunts I met in San Diego."

"Is that where you're from?"

I nodded, taking the plastic lid off my tea to let it cool faster. "I grew up near Camp Pendleton. My first two serious boyfriends were stationed there. Not at the same time," I added hastily.

"So you're a tag chaser from way back, huh?" The term was usually bandied about as an insult, but his soft smile let me know he'd meant no offense.

I smiled back. "What can I say? Apparently I'm a lifer. So, how'd you get from Baghdad to Boalt Hall?"

"The short version?" He sat back in his chair and took a deep breath. "I was separated from service last year under Don't Ask, Don't Tell."

Oh my God. "Someone outed you?"

"Sort of. I was a major in the infantry. My unit got rotated stateside to Camp Lejeune in North Carolina last summer. Time came to make recommendations for non-com promotions to my CO. I passed over this one guy, a real lazy fuck with a rotten attitude. Soon as he found out, he had it in for me."

He paused, sipped at his coffee. "About a month later, I took some leave time. Attended an anniversary dinner for two old friends who'd been honorably discharged from the Corps a few years earlier. Everyone was having a great time, laughing and drinking and telling stories. I stood up to make a toast with an old friend I'd had a brief fling with a few years back. The booze must've gotten the better of us, because we ended up kissing. The whole table started clapping, and guess who picked that exact moment to walk into the restaurant?"

"Shit."

"The second I saw the look on his face, I knew he was going to report me to our CO. When I got called into his office a few days later, I had my story all rehearsed and ready to go. But when I opened my mouth, the words wouldn't come. I just couldn't do it. I couldn't stand feeling so guilty when I'd done nothing wrong. I couldn't stomach perpetuating all the lies I'd told everyone, not to mention myself. It was my come-to-Jesus moment. I had no choice but to tell the truth."

For a second I wasn't sure I'd heard him right. I couldn't imagine Rob or Tony doing what Cole had done. Hell, they would've slashed their wrists first. "That was pretty damn brave."

"Or pretty damn stupid, according to my lawyer. He tried to get me to recant and claim I was under duress, but I wouldn't. I'd had it with making up stories about a girlfriend back home, being constantly on guard to keep from slipping up and saying the wrong thing. It was fucking exhausting. So, twelve years of my life, all those promotions and commendations, all flushed down the toilet. Once I said 'I'm gay,' the Corps acted as if none of it had ever happened."

My hand itched to slide across the table and clasp his, but I didn't dare. I didn't know him well enough to gauge how he'd react. Tony had freaked out the first time I'd tried to touch him in public. "So here you are, trying to reinvent yourself."

"I'd always planned to go to law school. Put in my twenty

years first, get my pension and the GI Bill. It just ended up happening sooner than I'd expected."

And obviously without Uncle Sam's help. "Did you get some kind of grant or scholarship?"

He didn't answer, and when I realized how nosy I'd sounded, I wanted to clap a hand over my mouth. "Sorry. None of my business."

"S'okay. I haven't really talked about this with anybody." He leaned in closer, his tone dropping to a murmur. "Just between you and me, my mama gave me the money. She inherited her parents' house a couple years ago, and she finally sold it. One day she walked into my room and handed me a check. Over a hundred grand. I tried to give it back, but she wouldn't hear of it. I told her I'd pay her back every dime. And I will if it's the last fucking thing I ever do."

"She sounds like quite a lady."

"She's got backbone, and no mistake. Being married to a hard-assed gunnery sergeant will help you grow one. Dad was none too pleased with her for giving me the money, but she told him he didn't get a vote. 'Course, he's none too pleased with me right now either. My discharge was a real slap in the face to him."

"That must've been rough." My throat was all tight and dry. I took a sip from my still-steaming cup to soothe it. "My mom's always accepted and loved me no matter what. Sometimes I forget it's not so easy for other people."

"No point whining over it. We play the hand we're dealt, right?"

"I guess."

We talked for well over an hour, segueing from the highlights of his life to mine and back again. Cole finally relaxed, laughing and smiling more easily. He had a thoughtful, almost courtly way about him that belied the usual macho

Marine image, along with a sly, dry sense of humor. The stories he told about the pranks and institutionalized hazing at the Academy had me gaping in disbelief. "My God, that's awful! How did you stand it?"

"I knew what to expect before I got there. Frankly, I would've been disappointed if they hadn't put me through hell. It made me a better Marine."

"Jesus. You guys are all such masochists." I glanced at the clock over the coffee bar, startled to see it was a quarter to nine. I still needed to get in a couple hours of writing before bed. Reluctantly, I pushed back my chair. "This has been great, but I should get going."

Cole nodded and scooped up our empty cups to toss in the trash, then followed me outside. "Mind if I see you home?" When I hesitated, he added with a smile, "Unless you don't want me to know where you live?"

Oh, this was silly. He already knew where I worked. It wasn't like he'd have a hard time finding me. "No, that's fine. I just wasn't expecting you to ask."

"We were having a nice conversation. I'm not ready for it to end yet."

I grinned. "Fair enough."

Three blocks south and two blocks east never went by so fast. Before I knew it, Cole was walking me up my front stairs. "Well," I said at the door, "good night."

A little divot formed between Cole's eyebrows. "So the date's over?"

I stared up at him, but in the haze of the porch light, I couldn't read what he was thinking. "For now, yeah."

"Okay." Falling back a step, he shoved both hands in his pockets. "Look, I'm not trying to crowd you. But I had a good time tonight, and I'd like to see you again."

Honest, straightforward, plain-spoken. I couldn't argue

with that. “I’d like to see you again too. But I don’t want a rerun of what happened last Sunday.”

“Neither do I.”

“Then why don’t we take it slow? Hang out for a while and see where it goes?”

“All right.” He smiled. “Although eventually I would like to get past your front door.”

A grin tugged at the corners of my mouth. “You know what they say about all good things.”

“I’ve got a feeling you’re worth waiting for.”

For a second I thought he was about to lean in and kiss me, but instead he scooped up my hand, brushed his lips across my palm and folded my fingers over it. “Hold onto that for me, okay?”

Then he tramped down the stairs and left me standing there, gaping at my hand. God, what was it about this guy? He had a knack for rendering me instantly stupid. Sure, we’d had a great time, but it was just one date. It’d take more than a cup of tea and a nice chat to erase the memory of last Sunday. At least, that’s what my sensible side said, though getting through to the rest of me was apparently another story.

I unlocked my door, stepped inside and slumped against it, my heart pounding for more reasons than I knew how to count.

Chapter 5

I didn't hear from Cole for the next few days, though between work and writing, I didn't spend much time dwelling on it. My current manuscript had taken off like a tornado, the words spilling out of my brain faster than I could type. This sort of thing didn't happen too often, so I stayed up 'til the wee hours trying to get it all down.

Friday morning I trudged into the diner, yawning and bleary-eyed, pulled my hair back into a stubby ponytail, put on my apron, and headed out front to help Terry with the breakfast crowd. She cocked her head toward the cash register the moment she saw me. "Your boyfriend dropped by and left you a little something."

Oh, God. He'd brought me *flowers*. One of those inexpensive bouquets of daisies, irises, and daffodils you could pick up at any grocery store, but still. He'd even put it in a vase with water. There was a card attached, too: *We forgot to exchange phone numbers the other night. Here's mine.* He'd scribbled it underneath. *Give me a call. Maybe we can do something this weekend? Best, Cole.*

I floated on air for the next couple hours, despite how busy it was. Finally we got a lull, and I headed out back to cool my heels for a minute. I pulled Cole's card out of my pocket and reread it, my idiotic grin warring with my depressingly rational urge to throw both the bouquet and the card in the nearest dumpster.

Of course Terry chose that exact moment to breeze into the kitchen for her latest order. "You two must've had a real nice date the other night."

"I told you, all we did was talk."

"Really? Then why'd he bring you the tried-and-true 'You were a great lay' present?"

I shot her a sour look. "He's a gentleman, Ter. He walked me to my door and everything."

"Huh. Didn't think they made 'em like that anymore." Her mouth dropped open. "Oh, my *God!* He's courting you old-school style! You lucky kid!"

I laughed. "I thought you didn't even like him."

"I'm exercising my womanly prerogative." She scooped up her plates and sashayed toward the door with a wink. "You sure he doesn't swing both ways?"

Snorting, I yanked out my phone and punched in Cole's number. Might as well thank him for his kind gesture. He picked up on the third ring. "Hey, it's Marc. I got your flowers."

"Yeah?" I could practically hear his shy smile. "You like 'em?"

"They're lovely. But you really didn't have to."

"It was the least I could do after you spent a whole evening listening to me bellyache."

"My pleasure." The line crackled with momentary silence. "So . . ."

"Um, yeah. I wondered if you wanted to do dinner or something? I can't afford anything too fancy, but—"

I hesitated. Why bother wasting time with someone who'd stop calling once he realized he might not get into my pants again? But still I opened my mouth and said, "Why don't you drop by the diner tonight? I get a free meal every four hours I work."

"You don't have to pay for me."

I bit my lip. Apparently I'd insulted his sense of pride. "It's no problem. You can pick up the tab next time, okay?"

"Well, all right." He did his best to sound gruff, but I could tell it was mostly an act. "Around seven, like last time?"

My answer stuck in my throat. I wanted to get to know Cole better, but . . .

Just because every other Marine I've dated turned out to be a jerk doesn't mean he'll be one too.

Well, okay, didn't mean he'd *still* be one.

"All right," I said. "It's a date."

I even knew exactly what to serve Cole for dinner. Idiotic grin reasserting itself, I hung up the phone, then went to talk to Fernando to make it happen.

Cole arrived at seven on the dot, but he looked tired, with purplish circles under his eyes and tight lines at the corners of his mouth.

"Rough day?" I asked, escorting him to our best table right next to the front window.

"Let's just say I'm glad it's over." He gave me a weary smile and sat down, eyebrows arching when I didn't follow suit. "Aren't you going to join me?"

"In a minute. But first, I've got a question for you." I paused a moment for effect. "Do you trust me?"

"With what? Ordering dinner? I'll have to think about it."

"Well, don't take too long, because our order's up." I headed to the kitchen to get it. Cole's big blue eyes went wide as the plates in my hand when I set his meal in front of him. Chicken-fried steak with mashed potatoes, country gravy, and fresh buttermilk biscuits.

He picked one up, pulled it apart, slathered it with butter and took a bite, letting out a soft, ecstatic groan as he chewed. "Homemade," he murmured. "I thought you didn't have 'em on the menu."

"We don't. But I sweet-talked Fernando into whipping up a batch."

"You did that for me?" God, he had such a sweet, utterly amazed look on his face, like a little kid who'd just gotten the bike he'd always wanted for Christmas.

"I figured you were due for a treat." I sat down across from him and dug into my Cobb salad. All conversation ground to a halt as we stuffed our faces.

The next time I looked up, every last morsel of food on Cole's plate was gone. "Wow, that was fast. You want seconds?"

I was joking, but for a moment there it looked like he was actually considering it. "Better not. But thanks. It was great." He covered his mouth to stifle a burp. "Best meal I've had since I got here."

"Who knew all it took was a heart attack on a plate to put a smile on your face?"

"That's not the only reason." He nudged his plate aside and rested his arms on the edge of the table. "It's nice having someone to talk to during dinner. Most nights I just heat up a can of soup or chili and eat it standing over the damn sink."

That had to be one of the saddest things I'd ever heard. "Haven't you made any other friends?"

"I've tried, but my schedule makes it pretty damn impossible. There's my classmates, but they're all focused on studying. The pace is fucking brutal. Hundreds of pages of reading every week, papers to write, midterms . . ." He sighed. "I'm barely keeping my head above water as it is."

"How about a study group? I wouldn't have gotten through grad school without one."

"Tried that too. Didn't make it through a single meeting before this guy got up in my face about the war. Said anybody who fought in Iraq was a government stooge. I came that close to knocking his fucking block off. After that, I figured I wasn't welcome back."

"That's Berkeley for you. People here are pretty liberal, and pretty outspoken about it."

"No shit. They sure as hell saw me coming."

"The haircut might've been their first clue," I said gently, hoping he wouldn't take it as another swipe at his pride. "Have you thought about letting it grow out?"

"That your way of saying you don't like it?"

Oh, God, if he only knew. The haircut, the uniform, the gung-ho attitude . . . it was all part of the turn-on for me. Had been ever since I was a teenager, watching those hot, hunky enlisted men swagger down the streets of San Diego.

"I like it," I admitted. "But a more conventional style might help you fit in."

"I've worn it this way for twelve years. I wouldn't recognize myself if I changed it." Another sigh. "And honestly, I don't want to change—my hair, or anything else. I want to go back."

Startled, I set down my fork. "Back to the Corps? You'd sign up again after the way they treated you?"

"In a heartbeat. Since I was ten, being a Marine's the only career I ever wanted. The only thing in my life that's ever mattered a damn to me."

It really shouldn't have surprised me. Rob and Tony had felt the same way. No matter how much abuse the Corps heaped on them, they were always right there, lining up for more. "That's what I call dedication." Or insanity, more like, but I wasn't about to say that aloud.

"Yeah, well, time to get my dedicated ass home and back to studying. I've got a paper due Monday that I've put off writing for the past week." He wadded up his napkin and tossed it onto his empty plate. "The frustrating part is, I know I'm not an idiot. I majored in economics at Annapolis. I've taken all kinds of advanced math and science classes. But every time I open one of my law books, it's like crashing into a brick wall.

And apparently I can't write worth shit anymore. I got a C on my last paper. A fucking C!"

A passing grade, but that plainly wasn't good enough for someone like Cole. I had to admire him for that. "If you need help, give me a call. I used to teach English."

"Really?" He smiled, eyebrows arching. "Well, thanks. I appreciate the offer."

We stood and walked up to the front counter, where I scribbled down my phone number and email address. His fingers closed over mine as I handed it to him, and a sweet little *zing!* went right through me. I had to clear my throat before I could say, "Good luck with the paper."

Just then, Terry barreled through the kitchen door, her laser-like gaze zeroing in on our clasped hands. Cole pulled his free of mine and mumbled, "Thanks for dinner," then zipped out the door so fast I could've sworn he'd left skid marks on the linoleum.

Are you *kidding* me? One person saw us touching and he ran for the hills?

Well, fuck that. Why hadn't I listened to my sensible side when it'd urged me to show him the door? Next time I'd know better.

CHAPTER 6

Saturday morning Cole rolled out of bed at oh-five-hundred, threw on his sweats, and headed out for a run. It was still dark, but the stars had long since faded, the sky faintly gray at the edges. He did his stretches and then started out at a jog, picking up the pace until the chill November air burned in his lungs.

He pushed past his customary five mile route, but not by much, reluctantly heading back before he lost too much time. He slowed the last half mile or so to cool down, and was pleasantly buzzed by the time he jogged up the front steps of his apartment building, clear-minded and focused on the rest of his day.

A hot shower and some plain black coffee, and he was ready to get back to studying. He sat down on the couch and fired up his laptop. No more putting off this damn paper. What was he was so fucking apprehensive about, anyway? It was a just case analysis—five pages, tops. Everybody else in his class could whip these things out in their sleep. He just needed to buckle down and do it.

But as usual, the words came slow as molasses in January. By noon, he'd only written a page and a half. Fighting down frustration and a rising sense of panic, he set his laptop aside and moved on to his required reading for contract law. Jesus, none of this made any fucking sense. His brain simply refused to absorb all these long Latin phrases and convoluted concepts. Why the hell had he ever thought law school was a good idea?

He was going to flunk out. Six more months of his life washed down the drain, just like the last twelve years.

On impulse, he grabbed his phone off the coffee table and hit speed-dial. It rang three times before Marc's voice echoed on the other end. "H'lo?"

"Hey. It's me." There came a loud clatter in the background, and Cole promptly winced. He'd obviously caught Marc at work. "Bad time?"

"No, it's fine. What can I do for you?"

He sounded strange. Stiff, formal, and not terribly friendly. A far cry from the warm, funny guy who'd bought him dinner last night. "Something wrong?"

"Of course not. Why would you think that?"

Okay, now he was laying it on with a trowel. "What'd I do this time?"

"I don't even know why you're calling. The way you left last night made everything pretty damn clear."

Huh? "I've got no fucking clue what you're talking about."

"Really? So that wasn't you tearing out of the diner like someone was chasing you?"

Oh. The immediate, jarring awareness of how he'd hurt Marc sent his stomach plummeting. "I'm sorry."

"You say that a lot."

"Look, I didn't mean to make you feel bad. For what it's worth, I didn't even realize I'd bolted 'til I was halfway down the block."

"And it never occurred to you to come back and apologize? Damn it, Cole, you acted like you were ashamed to be seen with me."

Shit. It seemed like every time they saw each other, he fucked it up. "I'm not ashamed, it's just . . . a reflex, I guess. I'm still getting used to the idea of not having to hide anymore. Don't you remember what it was like?"

"Not really," Marc said, icy cold. "I've been out since I was sixteen."

"Well, I envy you. Maybe someday I'll be as comfortable in my own skin as you are." He forced a smile, until he remembered Marc couldn't see him. "I really am sorry, you know. It won't happen again."

"Fine." Curt, but maybe not as upset as he was before. "So what were you calling me about?"

Well, at least he was willing to talk. "This damn paper's giving me fits. Been working on it all morning, and I've barely made any headway."

"Just calm down and focus. I'm sure you'll do fine."

"I'm not so sure. Hell, I'm not even sure I can hack it anymore. I thought this was what I wanted to do, but it's turned into a fucking nightmare."

"Look, everyone has a rough time in grad school at first. Even geeky brainiacs like me."

A shadow of a laugh colored Marc's tone—or was it just Cole's imagination? Maybe it was pushing his luck, but he had to find out. "Would you mind coming over to take a look at what I've got so far?"

"I'm sorry, but I need to get home and—"

"It won't take long. Hell, I've only got a couple pages written."

Marc hesitated. "All right. I get off work in an hour."

After they said their goodbyes, Cole tried to press on with his paper, but he ended up staring stupidly at the blinking cursor on his laptop. Time had never crept by so slowly.

His heart started thumping like a kettle drum when he finally heard a knock at the door. And there stood Marc, his green eyes shining, dark hair all messy and windblown. "Is it raining again?" Cole asked, holding out his hand for Marc's damp jacket.

"Sprinkling right now, but it's getting ready to pour. I don't want to walk home in it; I might have to hang out here for a while."

"Aw, damn." Cole grinned. "What a hardship."

"I thought you might say that." Marc wiped his rain-spattered glasses on his shirttail and nodded at Cole's laptop. "Well, c'mon. Let's take a look at this epic tome of yours."

The sky opened up outside, rain and wind lashing the windows as he and Marc worked away on the paper, huddled together over the laptop. Cole sat stiffly, trying not to let their knees touch or do anything that might seem too forward.

Eventually Marc turned to him and smiled, fingers closing over his sleeve. Cole smiled back, instantly relieved.

It was closing in on eight o'clock by the time Cole typed the last line, saved the file, and handed the laptop over to Marc for a final read-through. He stood up and stretched, his stomach grumbling. "Doesn't look like it's letting up out there. You want to order some pizza and watch a movie or something?"

"Or something?" Marc echoed, glancing up with a cute smile that made Cole want to turn cartwheels. "Sure, why not?"

The pizza joint was a couple blocks away, so even with the shitty weather, it only took about forty minutes to arrive. Cole got out plates, knives, forks, and beers while Marc rifled through his meager DVD collection.

"*Heartbreak Ridge*, *The Big Red One*, *Platoon*, *The Deer Hunter*. Hmm. I'm sensing a theme here."

Cole laughed. "So you like military guys, but not military movies?"

"I like military movies just fine, but don't you have anything made within, oh, the last twenty years? I mean, Clint Eastwood, for crying out loud!"

"What's wrong with Clint? He's a stud!"

"He's old enough to be my grandfather."

"Not in this one he isn't. Haven't you ever seen *Heartbreak Ridge*?"

Marc heaved a mock sigh and handed the disc over. "Go ahead, put it on."

Cole didn't have a DVD player, so he stuck the disc in his laptop and cued it up. The opening credits rolled as they dug into the double-cheese, double-pepperoni he'd ordered.

It'd been a while since Cole had watched this one himself. He'd always gotten a kick out of Eastwood's trademark macho swagger. The actor did a pretty good job nailing the rough and ready, my-way-or-the-highway attitude of every gunnery sergeant Cole had ever met—and one in particular.

"You okay?" Marc murmured, setting both of their empty plates on the table.

"Sure. Why wouldn't I be?"

"You're fidgeting."

"Oh." Hadn't even realized he was doing it. "Sorry. I forgot how much he reminded me of my father."

"You want to watch something else?"

"Nah, I'm fine." He stretched his arm along the back of the couch. Marc immediately stiffened, sat straight up. Cole pulled his arm back and scooted away. "Sorry."

Marc gave him a long look he couldn't quite figure out, then smiled and shook his head. "Stop apologizing, okay? C'mon back here."

This time Marc leaned in close, although Cole could still feel his muscles tensing. Well, Cole wasn't about to fuck things up again; he'd let Marc set the pace.

He tried to focus on the movie, which was pretty damn difficult once Marc rested his head gingerly on Cole's shoulder. A few more minutes, and Marc tucked his arm through Cole's. Cole followed suit, slumping back against the couch cushions. God, this felt good. Peaceful. *Right*. Alone together, with nothing to be afraid of. Not even the howl of the wind whipping through the trees outside, or the lights starting to flicker—

And blink out.

"Shit." Marc laughed nervously. "Wonder if the power's out at my place too?"

"Well, you're not gonna find out 'til the storm blows over. No way am I letting you walk home in this mess."

"Since when do you get to *let* me do anything?"

"Since you're a guest in my home, and I'm responsible for your safety."

"So you're gonna protect me from the elements, huh?" There was that cute smile again, beaming up at him in the pale light from the laptop screen.

They went back to watching the movie, but with the power out, it didn't take long for the battery to run down or the outside chill to seep in. Didn't bother Cole that much, but when Marc started to shiver, Cole sprang to his feet and made his way down the hall to the bedroom. He yanked the comforter off the bed and headed back to the couch, where he spread the blanket over both of them.

Marc tugged it up to his chin. "You could've just given me my jacket." He leaned close again, his head on Cole's shoulder. "But thanks."

"No problem." Even in the near-darkness, Cole could tell he was still smiling. It made him smile too. And then, on sheer impulse, he bent his head and kissed him.

Marc's lips were warm and soft, just like he'd imagined, opening under the gentle yet insistent push of his tongue—

Until Marc tore himself away a split-second later. "Jesus," Marc breathed. "Warn a guy, will you?"

"Sor—" No, he wasn't going to apologize this time. "I've been dying to do that since the night I took you out for coffee."

Marc stared down at the floor, arms crossed tightly over his chest.

"Relax, okay?" Cole put a hand on his shoulder, then slid it up to caress Marc's cheek. God, his pulse was thumping like a goddamn marching band. What the hell was he so afraid of? "I'm not gonna hurt you."

A short, bitter laugh, and then, "Not physically, at least."

Cole sat back, staring at him. "Christ, what kind of guys have you been dating?"

"Nobody special. That's the problem."

"I'm not planning to fuck you and forget you, you know."

Marc inched away, tensing as if he were about to stand. "No, actually, I don't. Though I can't figure out why you've gone to such trouble to get in my pants when you already got what you wanted from me the other day."

"Not everything I want from you. Not by a long shot." This time he forced himself to take it slowly, planting a chaste, cautious kiss on Marc's lips. Marc's breath froze, his fingers twisting in Cole's shirt. Was he trying to hold him tighter, or getting ready to push him away? Cole's heart lurched at the mere thought of the latter, but he kissed Marc's earlobe and whispered, "S'okay. Whatever happens next is up to you."

"This is a . . . a really bad idea."

"Why? I want you, and I think you want me too." He threw back the blanket, and gazed pointedly at Marc's erection. Cole could see it pulsing through the confines of Marc's jeans; he breathed deep, battling the urge to rip them right off him. "Doesn't this prove it?"

Yet the trepidation in Marc's eyes told another story.

"All right, I want you. But how do I know this won't end up a big fucking disaster?"

Again.

"Because this matters to me, Marc. *You* matter. But we won't know if it's worth it if we don't give it a chance. Look, I know I fucked up the other day. Let me make it up to you." Another kiss, gentle at first, then slow and deep, and this time it didn't take long for Marc's resistance to crumble. He started kissing Cole back, hands still curled in Cole's shirt as he slid sideways and stretched out on the couch, then tugged Cole on top of him.

Cole gazed down at Marc with a chuckle. "That's what I call getting into the spirit of things."

"Stop talking," Marc breathed, fingers wrapping around the back of Cole's skull to yank him down again.

Marc's moans echoed in Cole's ears as he slid his hands under Marc's shirt and pulled it over his head, then started to kiss a warm, wet path down his torso. God, his skin felt so fucking good, soft and smooth except for a small patch of crisp dark hair at the center of his chest. A few extra pounds around his waist, but that was fine. Cole had seen too many starving people in his travels to find rail-thinness attractive anymore. Cole's cock ached, straining against his fly, but he did his best to ignore it. Last Sunday had been all about him. Tonight it was all about Marc.

He eased down Marc's zipper and reached inside, freeing his cock. Slick pre-cum already coated the tip, and Cole sucked it into his mouth, its flavor exploding on his tongue. Marc let loose a gasp and grabbed hold of the bristly half-inch of hair on top of Cole's head, but Cole shook him off. He'd only done this in alleyways or men's rooms in sleazy bars, where "quick and dirty" were the watchwords. He'd never had a chance to enjoy the experience before.

So he settled in and took his time, savoring the thick weight of Marc's cock on his tongue. Every lick, flick, and swirl coaxed little groans and broken whimpers out of Marc that told Cole he was getting close. He considered sucking him to the edge, then easing off and starting all over again, but he suspected Marc would strangle him if he tried. Besides, he couldn't fucking *wait* to taste him.

Marc's gasps and cries quickly melded into one word—"*ColeColeCole*"—over and over. A sharp thrill of pride snaking through him, Cole sucked harder, faster, until Marc came with a sweet little shout. So damn *good.* So much better than in all those bars—hell, a hundred times better, because it was Marc. He swallowed it all down, then pulled off, grinning his pleasure when Marc tugged him up for a kiss. Hot, sticky, brain-meltingly intimate. He'd never done that before, either.

They were both panting by the time they broke apart, hearts still pounding. "What about you?" Marc whispered.

Cole groaned, resting his forehead against Marc's. "I really, *really* wish I could fuck you right now."

"Well, your wish is about to be granted." Marc reached over and started working on Cole's zipper, until Cole closed his hands over Marc's and made him stop. "What're you doing? I thought you wanted to—"

"We can't. Not tonight, anyway. I don't have any condoms. Or lube."

"Oh." Marc blinked at him, then let out a bark of nervous laughter. "I was afraid you were gonna tell me you had herpes or something."

Ouch. "Why? Because Marines'll screw anything that moves?"

"You know that's not what I meant," Marc said gently, sitting up. "Look, it's not the end of the world. There are plenty of other things we can do. Fun things. *Hot* things."

"Hotter than blowjobs?"

"Oh, *hell* yeah. Now get those pants off."

Just as Cole scrambled to his feet and started unbuttoning his fly, there came a loud *crack-pop* outside, and the room flickered with bright white light. Cole dropped to his knees and crouched down low, covering his head. Adrenaline surged through his veins at another near-blinding flash.

"Hey," came a voice from right above him, gentle fingers closing over his shoulder, rubbing his back. "Don't be scared. It's just lightning."

A familiar rumble echoed in the distance, followed by another a few seconds later. Thunder, not bombs. He was in his own living room, not Baghdad or Fallujah. *Oh, holy fuck*. If there'd been enough space under the couch, he'd have crawled into it gratefully. Good thing the room had gone dark again. Maybe Marc wouldn't notice how fucking mortified he was.

"Sorry," he murmured, wincing at the apology, even though this one was definitely warranted. Shivering, he took Marc's hand and let him pull him back up onto the couch and tug the blanket over him.

Marc's arms went around him, holding him close, one hand sliding up to stroke his hair. A simple gesture of kindness and comfort, yet it came that close to breaking Cole in half. Was this what he'd been reduced to—accepting someone else's protection? That was supposed to be *his* job. He dragged in a shaky breath, one after another, until the worst of it passed.

"Sorry," he said again.

"Take it easy," Mark murmured. "It's nothing I haven't seen before. You're not the first Marine I've dated, remember?"

"Even so, I thought you would've been out the door by now."

"Give me a little credit. I don't scare that easily."

They sat back together with Marc's head on Cole's shoulder again, one of Marc's hands tracing idly over Cole's chest. Warm, steadying and reassuring. Exactly what he needed.

"Does this kind of thing happen often?" Marc asked.

"Not as much as it used to, but . . . Well, it's not like I can control it." He tried to relax, but even with Marc touching him, there was nothing stirring below his belt. Figured. After what'd just happened, he'd need a forklift to get it up again. "Talk about killing the mood, huh?"

"Don't worry about it."

"You mean I didn't mess this up so bad you never want to see me again?"

"Will you stop trying to second-guess me? God, you Marines are all such fucking control freaks." He pulled back to look at Cole. "Listen, Thanksgiving's next Thursday. Why don't you come over to my place? I'll cook us dinner, and we can spend the whole afternoon and evening together. And all night too, if you want. No pressure either way. Unless you already have plans?"

Cole smiled. "Other than sleeping for four days? Nope, no plans at all."

They sat together in the dark, listening to the storm rage outside. There were more flashes of lightning, but Marc's calming warmth pressed up next to him kept him from freaking out again. Obviously somebody up there was looking out for him, but now it was up to him to make the next time count. To not screw it up.

So much for no pressure.

Chapter 7

By the time Thursday rolled around, I was really starting to wonder what the hell I'd gotten myself into. I'd never cooked Thanksgiving dinner by myself before, although I'd helped my mom with plenty of holiday meals over the years. I enjoyed cooking, but there wasn't much point getting fancy about it when it was just me. Still, I wanted the day—and the evening—to be damn near perfect. Which meant all the planning was stressing me out.

I ended up ordering a twelve-pound organic turkey, pre-stuffed with mushroom and sage dressing. I would've preferred doing it myself, but my tiny kitchen wasn't designed for such ambitious projects. Counter space was at such a premium, I had to peel potatoes on my postage-stamp-sized kitchen table.

Afterward, I showered and shaved, then stood in front of my closet stark naked for ten fucking minutes trying to decide what to wear. A nice, conservative cashmere sweater, or something that screamed, "What're you waiting for? *Fuck* me already!"? I settled on my newest, cleanest non-work jeans and a plain white v-neck t-shirt that clung in all the right places. Simple, classic—and easy to get out of in a hurry.

With his usual military precision, Cole showed up on my doorstep at one-thirty on the dot, sporting a huge grin and a suspicious-looking pink box. "What's this?" I asked, nodding at the box as I ushered him inside. "I only asked you to bring a bottle of wine."

"Which I did." He pulled a brown paper bag out from under his arm. "The guy at the wine store said either zinfandel or pinot noir was a good choice with turkey, so I went with the pinot. Hope that's okay."

From the label, it looked like a standard California pinot. Nothing fancy, but that was fine. "You still haven't answered my question. What's in the box?"

His grin widened as he slowly lifted the lid. I peered inside, and my jaw dropped. "Oh, my God! Pumpkin cheesecake from Sandrine's! It's my favorite! How the hell did you *know?*"

"A little bird named Terry let it slip. She said to tell you to save her a piece."

"Screw that! In fact, screw the turkey. I might just have this for dinner." I set it in the fridge, right next to the cartons of candied yams, green bean casserole, and cranberry sauce I'd picked up at the grocery store. "Well, okay, maybe not. But thank you."

"I think I deserve a kiss, don't you?" He wrapped his arms around me before I could get out another word, kissing me so long and deep it left me dizzy. The spicy scent of Hugo Boss cologne crept up my nostrils, and it was all I could do to keep from climbing him like a fucking rock wall.

Breathless, head still spinning, I tore myself away. Our first kiss in full daylight. I wasn't sure I'd survive another one. "That was . . ."

"Intense?" he supplied, worrying at my lower lip with the pad of his thumb. Just like he'd done that Sunday we'd met, right before I sank to my knees to suck him off.

(Right before he kicked you out without a by-your-leave.)

Eleven days ago. Felt more like six months.

Cole smiled down at me, and I forgot all about— well, whatever it was I'd been thinking about. "You've got no idea," he said, "how much I want to throw you down and take you right now."

"My bed's in the next room. Let's go." I grabbed his hand

and tried to drag him along, but he refused to budge. "What's the problem? You trying to get me back for that night I wouldn't let you come in?"

"We've waited this long, we can wait a couple more hours." He pulled me close again, cradling my face in his hands. His eyes were so damn blue I could've fallen in and drowned. God knew I wanted to. "Why don't you give me the nickel tour?"

Nickel was right, in that it took about five minutes. He seemed fascinated by my workspace, especially the postcards with my book covers on them tacked up over my desk. "J.M. Sullivan," he read aloud. "What's the 'J' stand for? Or is it just a made-up pen name?"

"No, it's real. James Marcus. But I've always gone by Marc."

He looked closer, and I knew what he was going to ask next before he even opened his mouth. "So you wrote all these? And they're romance novels? With two *guys?*"

"One of 'em's got *three* guys."

"You're kidding. You mean, you actually make money at this?"

I'd been afraid he'd mock me when he found out, but he looked more amazed, even admiring, than anything else. "Not a whole lot, but I've only been at it a couple years. Takes a while to build up a following. Hence my day job at the diner."

There followed an awkward momentary silence with us both trying not to look at the bed—until a familiar black furry head popped out from under it and mewed.

"Who's this?" Cole promptly dropped to a crouch, holding out his hand. Thomas crept toward him and gave his fingers a cautious sniff, then began licking them. "He's sure friendly."

"His name's Thomas. I named him after the cat I had in high school."

"I had a cat back then too—or rather, my mama did. A chocolate-point Siamese named Samba. For some reason, she took a real shine to me. Slept at the foot of my bed and everything. Mama said after I left for the Academy, she sat outside my bedroom door crying every morning for two damn months. Silly beast, but she sure was sweet. Just like this little guy." He gave Thomas's ears a final scritch, then straightened up. "So when's dinner? I'm starving."

With the savory aroma of roasting turkey and dressing floating through the air, my stomach started to growl too. Then it twisted into mortified knots when we went back in the kitchen and I saw I still needed to clear all the food prep off the table. "Sorry. I'm not usually so disorganized," I said, dashing over to take care of it.

Cole hung back until I got out the plates, knives, forks, and wine glasses. "Why don't you let me set the table while you get the food ready?" he said. It was apparently a rhetorical question, because he scooped everything out of my hands before I could reply.

Between the two of us, we managed to get everything ready before we keeled over from hunger. My table was nowhere near big enough to hold all the dishes, so we left the roasting pan on top of the stove, set everything else on the counter, and served ourselves buffet-style. Thomas was *very* interested in the turkey, so I put a few morsels in his bowl before finally plopping down at the table.

Cole poured us some wine and raised his glass with a smile. "Thanks for inviting me. Happy Thanksgiving."

I smiled back. "Happy Thanksgiving." We clinked and drank to it, then dug in like a pair of starving lumberjacks.

"So," Cole asked at last, after he'd polished off his first plateful and gotten up for seconds, "how old were you when you, um . . ."

"Knew I was gay?"

He nodded as he sat back down, loaded plate in hand. "If you don't mind me asking."

"No, it's fine. Honestly, I can't remember a time when I didn't know there was something different about me. Even when I watched movies or TV as a kid, I always found the guys more attractive than the women. It wasn't until I got to high school that I realized what it all meant."

"Must've been nice to get it figured out so early. I can't remember being anything but confused about my orientation until I was, God, nineteen or twenty."

"Did you ever date women?"

"I had a girlfriend in high school, but we never slept together. Our families were both pretty religious, so we had the 'no premarital sex' lecture drummed into us from early on. We actually did get engaged before I left for the Academy, but I broke it off the following summer. All it took was being around gorgeous men in uniform twenty-four seven to make me realize why I'd never wanted to have sex with her." He refilled both our glasses, then took a long sip from his own. "Jen's married with kids now, but we've stayed good friends. I think she always knew what was up with me, even though she never said a word. She was the only member of our church who dropped by my place to see me after my discharge."

I didn't know whether to cry at that or put my fist through the nearest wall. Instead I reached across the table to clasp his hand, absurdly pleased when he not only let me, but actually entwined our fingers.

"If it's any consolation," I replied, "California's generally more liberal in its attitudes toward gays than North Carolina. Certain ballot initiatives notwithstanding."

"So I've noticed, but it's still not home."

I smiled. "Give it time, and maybe we can change that."

Cole loaded up the dishwasher while I packaged up the leftovers and put them in the fridge. He came up behind me as I was setting the empty roasting pan in the sink, wrapped his arms around my waist, and backed me up against the counter to kiss me long, slow, and deep enough to render me momentarily stupid. *Again*.

"I think we've waited long enough, don't you?" he murmured.

Oh, *fuck*, yes.

Off came our shoes and socks, littering the floor from kitchen to living room. But when Cole started to yank his t-shirt over his head, I grabbed hold of his wrists to stop him. "Not so fast, Marine. I've been fantasizing about that gorgeous bod of yours for the past week and a half. The least you can do is stand there and let me unwrap it."

One beautiful blond eyebrow arched. "Is that an order?"

"Yeah." I grinned. "I believe it is."

"Well, in that case . . ." He obligingly lifted his arms over his head.

My fingertips had skimmed those six-pack abs in the dark the other night, but seeing them for the first time made my mouth go desert-dry. The rest of him was no disappointment either. I smoothed both hands slowly up his torso, savoring the feel of each muscle. They pulsed under his skin like living steel, ropy and powerful but not the least bit grotesque. A body built with sweat and hard work, not steroids.

His cock popped right up the second I got his fly undone, this time without any pesky boxers in the way. "Commando, huh?" I wrapped my fingers around him and gave a few quick strokes, chuckling at Cole's sharp gasp. "That was considerate. Or maybe you just haven't done this week's laundry yet?" I stepped back. "Take 'em off and turn around. I want the full view."

Oh, Christ. Solid, tree-trunk thighs, shapely calves—and a round, sculpted ass that belonged in a fucking museum. Michelangelo's *David* had nothing on Cole. Just looking at him made me lightheaded. I backed up slowly and sank down on the foot of the bed. "I-I feel like I've just won the lottery."

"And instead of millions, I'm your prize?" Cole turned to face me, sporting a surprised grin. "Hope you're not disappointed."

"Are you kidding? Haven't you ever looked in a mirror?" Jesus, was he actually *blushing?* "Who needs millions when I've got a Nordic god in my bedroom?"

"I'm not a god. I'm just a guy." He dropped to his knees in front of me and laid his head in my lap. "And spending today with you has made me happier than I've been in a long, long time."

God, this had all happened so fast. What the hell was I thinking, inviting him into my home and my bed when we barely knew each other? The rational part of my brain screamed at me to put on the brakes right now, but the other part—the part that wanted to wrap my legs around him and never let him go—clapped a hand over its mouth. "I hope *you're* not disappointed."

"Not a chance." He caught hold of my hand and kissed my fingertips one by one, then pushed me back on the bed.

Between the two of us, we got my clothes and glasses off and peeled back the covers, rolling together skin to skin on cool white cotton. I longed to memorize every cut, ripple, and divot on Cole's body with my lips and tongue, but evidently he had the same idea. He pinned me to the mattress and proceeded to kiss me all over, burying his face in my armpits and the crease between my thigh and groin. Then he opened wide and swallowed my cock as if it were his last meal.

He had me hovering on the brink in nothing flat; I had

to push hard on his shoulders to get him to stop. "Not yet," I panted. "Not 'til you're inside me."

He rolled to his feet and snatched his jeans up off the floor, rummaging in his pockets for condoms and lube. But his hands trembled so badly he couldn't get the condom wrapper open. I snatched it from him and tore the foil with my teeth. The condom popped right into my mouth. I promptly leaned over, using my lips to slide it onto the tip of his cock, then as far down as I could go without choking.

"Jesus," Cole hissed with a sharp, startled laugh, "where the hell did you learn to do *that?*"

I shot him an enigmatic grin and gave him a quick squeeze at the root to make sure our encounter didn't end too quickly. The tight, desperate look on his face made it plain he was already on the ropes.

Time to give him something else to concentrate on. "C'mon, get me ready," I said, spreading my thighs as I pressed the tube of lubricant into his hand. I would've preferred it if he'd rimmed me first, but I doubted either of us would last long enough for that.

Maybe he hadn't done this in a while, but like riding a bike, he obviously hadn't forgotten how. Those long fingers of his worked a generous dollop of lube inside me, then quickly slicked his cock. God, his hands were still shaking. Had I really done that to him? *Me?*

My breath caught as he pressed the tip of his dick against my hole and pushed in slowly. He was long and thick, so it hurt at first, but not as much as I'd expected. He didn't move right away, other than to stretch out on top of me and start kissing my chest and throat.

"Jesus, you feel like fucking heaven," he whispered. "I'm afraid if I do anything, I'll wake up and discover this whole week and a half's been a dream."

So tough on the outside, but on the inside he was all marshmallow. My heart cracked wide open for him. "I'm right here." I kissed the crown of his head and rolled my hips, until we both gasped in unison. "And I'm sure as hell not a dream."

His blue gaze met mine, and the sheer startling intimacy of that look made me moan. He started to move, slow and deep at first, then more rapidly. Soon he was slamming me into the mattress so hard I knew I'd be bruised from navel to knees tomorrow, but I didn't fucking *care.* I never wanted him to stop.

Wave after wave of pleasure washed over me, a maelstrom whirling in my head. Too much. He had me on the knife's edge, so sharp it threatened to flay me. I let my eyes drift shut and hung on.

"Don't do that," Cole said, his voice all sexily raspy and hoarse, just like last Sunday at his place. Just like during the storm the other night. "C'mon, stay with me. We're almost there."

I didn't think it was possible for him to fuck me harder, but he did, every thrust pushing me across the mattress until my head lolled over the side. For a second I was afraid I'd tumble right off, but Cole grabbed my shoulders and pulled me back up. He gave me that *look* again and swooped in for a rough, savage kiss, one hand tangling in my hair, and that was it—I went flying, every cell in my body pulsing.

Cole followed quickly after, smothering his broken roar in my mouth, collapsing atop me for one blissfully hot, sticky moment before rolling off. Took him a minute to catch his breath, and then he sat up and pounded his fists on his chest like King Kong.

I burst out laughing. I couldn't help it. "You're crazy!"

"Nope, just happy." He grabbed a handful of tissues from the box on the bedside table and cleaned us both off, then laid down and pulled me over next to him.

I wrapped my arm around his waist, even as that tiny, sensible voice at the back of my mind gave me a brisk scolding. I closed my eyes and told it to shut the fuck up.

CHAPTER 8

I woke up alone, a sound I couldn't quite make out echoing from the next room. Every muscle in my body screamed as I rolled out of bed, snagged my jeans from the floor, and yanked them on. I padded into the kitchen to find Cole hunched over the sink scrubbing out the roasting pan, whistling an off-key tune I belatedly recognized as "Jingle Bells."

I giggled. "Christmas carols? To wash dishes by?"

"It was either that or the Marine Corps hymn. Didn't figure you'd want to wake up to 'Halls of Montezuma.'" He flashed me a grin and wiped his hands on a towel before coming over to give me a kiss. "'Morning, by the way. Man, you were really tired. I've been up an hour already."

He was actually surprised? Christ, we'd gone at it half the night, and Cole probably would've kept going if I hadn't conked out on him. He had the most amazing stamina of any guy I'd ever been with. It was like being fucked by the love child of Superman and the Energizer Bunny.

Not that I was complaining, especially when he had enough energy left over to clean my kitchen the next morning. Every surface practically *glowed*. And I was still getting over the fact that he was here. I'd half-expected to wake up with nothing but a Cole-sized dent in the mattress. "It wasn't this clean when I moved in. But I didn't ask you over to do housework, you know."

"Hey, you cooked. It was the least I could do to finish cleaning up. Besides, me and my pal Thomas were hanging out, getting to know each other better. Weren't we, buddy?" Thomas lounged on one of the kitchen chairs, licking his paws.

He cast his lazy green gaze upward as Cole came over to pet him. "He seemed hungry, so I gave him a little kibble and a couple bits of turkey. I hope that's okay."

"You're an easy touch. He's always hungry. He'd weigh twenty pounds if I fed him every time he begged for it."

"Speaking of which . . ." Cole ambled back and wrapped his arms around me. "Say the word, and I'd be happy to fall to my knees right now."

The memory of what that mouth and tongue could do made me all quivery. I was sorely tempted to unzip my jeans and let him have at it, but a glance at the clock over the sink dashed my hopes. "I have to be at work in forty-five minutes."

"Aw, damn." He gave me another kiss and a wistful smile. "You want a cup of tea? Or I could whip up some eggs while you're in the shower."

With any other guy, such eagerness to please might've come off as pushy, but with Cole I found it sweet, even touching. Too bad I had to turn him down. "That's okay. I'm not much of a breakfast eater. I'll grab something at the diner later."

"All right. I should be getting home anyway. I need to go out on my run, then I've got a shitload of reading to do."

I followed him into the other room and watched while he sat down on the bed to put his shoes on. I hadn't even realized he was stomping around barefoot. Made me glad he felt comfortable enough to do that. One night together, and the thought of him leaving already bummed me out.

"Look, you're welcome to stay for the rest of the weekend," I said, tempted to kick myself the second the words had left my mouth. Way to sound all overeager and needy.

"Yeah?" Eyebrows raised, Cole finished tying his laces and stood. "You sure?"

Jesus, he actually *wanted* to? "Yeah. Bring your books and your laptop, and you can study while I'm at work. It's nice and quiet here. You and Thomas will have plenty of time to bond."

Then I remembered Ben and I had plans for a critique session on Saturday. But that was okay. Ben was pretty easygoing. I'd give him a call later to reschedule. "Besides," I added, "someone's got to help me eat all those leftovers." There was an extra front door key hanging on a peg by the stove. I snagged it and handed it to him. "Let yourself in. I'll be home a little after seven."

"Sounds good," he replied with a grin, slipping on his leather jacket—that tight black leather jacket that sent all kinds of kinky thoughts dancing through my perverted smut-writer's brain. Like shoving him back on the bed so I could sit on his dick. Instead, I stood there like an idiot and let him kiss me goodbye.

It didn't even occur to me to call in sick until after I heard his footsteps clomp downstairs and fade away. No, I'd better not. I couldn't afford to lose a day's worth of tips. Besides, Terry would skin me alive if I left her to face all those ravenous Black Friday shoppers alone.

A hot shower and my regular stroll to the diner helped loosen my stiff muscles a bit, but Terry's eyes still raked me up and down like a searchlight as I limped into the kitchen to put on my apron. "You're moving kind of slow this morning. Guess all that cheesecake's weighing you down, huh?"

Oh, God. I'd forgotten all about the damn cheesecake. "We never got around to having any."

"Well, sounds like you two had a happy holiday." She flashed me a big, sincere smile. "You got yourself a handsome hunk of man with some real romance in his soul. It was so adorable, the way he came in to quiz me about all your favorite stuff the other day. I envy you, kiddo." With a wink, she stacked her order along her arm and headed out front. "But I want *details* later!"

Later never materialized. The steady flow of customers kept us both hopping all day, with barely enough time to scarf down a sandwich. Usually I didn't mind when it was busy, even insanely busy. It made the time go by more quickly. But today, all I wanted was to go home and be with Cole, so naturally the last couple of hours crawled by like a constipated snail. At last, around a quarter to seven, Terry clapped me on the shoulder. "Go on, loverboy. I can take it from here."

Sore muscles notwithstanding, I motored home pretty fast. I'd expected to find Cole at the kitchen table eating or studying, but there was only his backpack slung over a chair. Then I heard a soft, raspy snore and poked my head around the corner. Cole lay stretched out on the bed with Thomas curled up at his side and a textbook open on his lap. It was so damn cute I pulled out my phone to take a picture.

Cole's eyes opened the moment I snapped it. "Hey, you're back." He shoved his book aside and patted the mattress. "C'mere." I laid down next to him while Thomas, mightily peeved at having his slumber disturbed, gave us both a dirty look, stretched, and stalked off.

"Busy day?" Cole asked, wrapping his arm around me.

"Yeah, but it's over. Thank God." I sighed. "Did you get a lot of studying done?"

"Actually, I did. Amazing what a little relaxation will do for your state of mind. Maybe I should read in bed all the time."

"Well, as much as I adore a well-read man, I can think of a few other things I'd rather be do—" My empty stomach rumbled, and I bit my lip in a vain attempt at stifling my embarrassment. "Oops."

Cole just laughed and rolled to his feet, pulling me along with him. "Sounds like we should dig into those leftovers."

We devoured them in short order, chasing our meal down with the remaining half-bottle of pinot. Cole insisted we try the cheesecake this time, but it was so rich I only managed a couple of bites before pushing my plate away.

"That's all? You were making some serious yummy noises

there," Cole said. "From the way Terry talked about how much you loved this stuff, I thought you'd be carrying on like it was better than sex."

I chuckled, breaking eye contact as highlights from our romp last night flickered through my brain. I still couldn't believe he was sitting across the table from me. What had happened to the skittish, panicky guy who'd turned tail and ran the night Terry had seen us holding hands?

"So why hasn't some lucky man snapped you up by now?" Cole asked. "Those other Marines must've been out of their fucking minds to let you slip through their fingers."

"That was a long time ago. I was younger, and stupider. I put up with a lot of shit I shouldn't have." I scooped up my wine glass and swirled it, trying to decide whether to tell him the rest. Might as well get it over with. At least that way if I scared him off, I wouldn't be too used to having him around yet.

I knocked back my last sip of wine and said, "You remind me a little of Tony. He was really conflicted about his feelings the entire time we were together. I mean, he said he loved me in private, but he was scared to death of anybody seeing us out together. He went home for Christmas swearing he was going to come out to his family and that when his enlistment was up in six months, we'd move in together and everything would be sunshine and roses."

"I take it that didn't happen," Cole prompted.

"He freaked out and eloped to Vegas with some woman he used to date back home. I thought he was joking when he called to tell me. When I realized he was serious, I lost it. I yelled loud enough to peel paint off the walls. I'm pretty sure the whole neighborhood heard."

"Did they applaud?"

"No, but my mom did. She never liked him. But then, she liked Rob, and that didn't turn out much better." Thomas chose that moment to come give me his patented "I'm hungry" look, complete with big eyes and a mournful meow. Against my better judgment, I scraped the few scattered morsels of turkey left on my plate into his bowl. Who was the easy touch now?

"Is there more to the Rob story, or do I have to guess?" Cole asked, getting up to fill our empty wine glasses with tap water.

I waited until he handed mine back before continuing. "Rob was a hundred and eighty degrees different from Tony. We met in a West Hollywood bar, for God's sake—that's about as out as you can get and still be a Marine. We were together almost a year. Then one Sunday, he called to tell me he was being transferred. He couldn't say where. That was the last time I ever heard from him." I blinked against the memory, the pain still surprisingly fresh. Why had I drunk my wine so quickly?

"That sucks," Cole murmured. "And I always thought it was so much easier for you civilian guys."

"That's the thing about loving men in uniform. Eventually you all go away."

He reached for my hand. "I'm not going anywhere. The Corps doesn't want me anymore. And I made up my mind today that this law school thing's not going to beat me."

Wow. Talk about a complete one-eighty. "What brought this on? The other day you told me you didn't think you could hack it."

"That was just me wallowing in self-pity. I thought I was in this alone. Now I know I'm not." He smiled. "Feels good having someone else in my corner for a change."

"Well, I'm flattered, but don't pin all your hopes on me. You're the one who has to do the work."

He squeezed my fingers. "Look, if I can graduate with honors from Annapolis and survive five fucking tours in the sandbox, no way am I letting a few textbooks and term papers kick my ass. As far as I'm concerned, I'm here for the duration. Okay?"

I wanted to believe him, I really did. And when he pulled me to my feet and kissed me, then led me back to bed, I wanted that too. I let him undress me, the way I'd done with him last night, standing as still as I could while he tugged off my shirt and jeans. He dusted kisses over my skin as he went.

"You're sweet to make such a fuss," I whispered once we'd crawled under the covers. "But you really don't have to."

His forehead crinkled. "What're you talking about?"

"Compared to yours, my body's nothing to crow about. I keep meaning to get to the gym, but somehow I never find the time."

"Don't be silly. You're perfect."

"You should've met me before I started working at the diner. I've gained a few pounds since then, most of it on my ass."

"Hey, I like a round, plush ass. Gives more cushion for the pushin'. Allow me to demonstrate." He rolled me onto my stomach, but rather than touch my ass, he started massaging my shoulders and kissing the nape of my neck.

His strong hands worked the knots out of my sore muscles and dissolved me into a warm, contented puddle. I'd just begun to drift off when I realized we hadn't gotten to the main event yet. I started to turn over, but Cole pressed his hand to the center of my back. "S'okay. Go to sleep."

What? He was done with me already? "But don't you want to—"

"Sure I do, but you're tired. We don't have to rattle the walls every night." His lips brushed my shoulder again, then he spooned behind me and yanked the covers up over us.

He started snoring a few minutes later, but by then I was wide awake, my ego smarting over his sweet but rather puzzling rejection. His fading erection prodding my back told me he hadn't lied about wanting to fuck me. Oh, Jesus, what was I complaining about? He was obviously just trying to be considerate, which was more than I could say for the majority of guys I'd dated.

And that's what worried me. In my experience, smooth sailing usually meant some awful storm was looming up ahead. No point in agonizing over it now, though. Might as well enjoy what fun Cole and I were having for as long as it might last.

Chapter 9

Heading back to class Monday morning was kind of a bummer after four days with Marc, but for once Cole didn't actively dread it. He took his regular seat at the rear of the lecture hall, nodding at the blonde girl in wire-frame glasses who usually sat in the same row. Sandra, that was her name. Or was it Sondra?

"You must've had a nice weekend," she commented, opening her laptop. "This is the first time I've seen you smile all semester."

He was smiling? He had to rub a hand over his face to make sure. Not just smiling, but grinning like some loopy moron. Strangely enough, he didn't care who noticed.

His good mood refused to dissipate even when the professor stepped up to the podium and started droning on about writs of *habeas corpus* and *certiorari*. Last week, Cole would've already been drumming his fingers on the desk and checking his watch. But now, for the first time he could remember, the class seemed to zip by. Soon the professor drew to a close, assigned some reading, and told everyone to expect their graded case analysis papers emailed back to them that afternoon.

Cue butterflies. Still, he had no real reason to be worried about this one. Marc had helped him with it, and he thought it deserved at least a B. Nothing to do now but cross his fingers and wait.

Luckily, Mondays were a short day. His constitutional law class was over at noon, so he decided to go home for lunch.

Then he remembered there was nothing in his fridge except a six-pack of beer. He hadn't bothered going grocery shopping last week after Marc had invited him over for Thanksgiving dinner.

He swung by a little mom-and-pop corner market and picked up a few essentials before heading home. There was a U-Haul parked in front of his building, which wasn't all that surprising, since it was the end of the month. But the two scruffy, skinny, dreadlocked guys wrangling a ratty-looking couch down the truck's back ramp were definitely moving *in*, not out.

And they were moving in on his floor—right across the hall, in fact, if all the grunting and bumping noises wafting through the half-open door were any clue. Oh, great. This didn't bode well for his peace and quiet.

Cole finished putting away his groceries, then sat down to check his email. Still no word on his paper. He opened his textbook and started to read, but now he couldn't concentrate. His fingers tingled, that familiar old knot of anxiety congealing in his chest. Evidently, this morning's cheerful mood had been a temporary aberration. Xanax would help, but he hadn't taken any in over a week, and he didn't want to get back in the habit. Besides, he didn't have any refills left, so he needed to make them last as long as he could. Maybe another run would do the trick.

As he threw on his sweats, something crashed outside his apartment door. He yanked it open to find the two skinny dreadlocked guys struggling to get a queen-sized mattress down the hall. They'd apparently given up on carrying it and were now trying to turn it end over end.

Shit. It'd take them forever, and they were already blocking his way out. "Let me give you a hand here," Cole said, grabbing one of the short ends of the mattress while indicating with a jerk of his chin for the other two guys to take up the opposite end. Between the three of them they got it upright, then toted it the few remaining feet down the hall and into the other apartment's bedroom.

"Thanks for helping, man," the shorter, blonder guy said, wiping his forehead on his sleeve before extending his hand. "I'm Jerry, by the way."

"Kumar," supplied the other guy with a nod.

"Pleased to meet you," Cole replied. "Next time remember to lift with your legs, okay? You don't want to throw your backs out before you even get moved in."

Jerry and Kumar traded a "no shit" look as the three of them ambled back out to the living room. There was another guy putting stuff away in the kitchen, banging every fucking cupboard door as he went. This apartment had the same floor plan as Cole's, which meant the couch took up most of the available space—except for the drum kit wedged in the living room's far corner. Right next to the huge amplifier.

Holy fuck. "I didn't realize Led Zeppelin was moving in next door," Cole said, pasting on what he hoped wasn't the world's fakest-looking smile.

"Yeah, we were lucky to find this place on such short notice," Jerry answered cheerfully. "Our last landlord was a dick, but the management here seems really nice. There's not too many apartments we can afford with a living room big enough for all four of us to practice in."

"That many, huh?" He bit his cheek. "But you're not all living here, right?"

"No, no, just me and Kumar. Although the other guys might stay over on show nights. We just landed a weekend gig at this new club on the other side of campus. You should come hear us sometime."

"Oh, I'm sure I'll be hearing a lot from you," Cole replied with a wave, beating a quick retreat. Terrific, just fucking *terrific*.

Now he'd be lucky if he ever got another wink of sleep.

Fortunately, his forty-minute run left him calmer and more focused. He took a shower, then changed into clean clothes and padded back to the living room to check his email.

And there it was—a message from the professor's teaching assistant with his graded paper attached. Cole sucked in a breath and opened it. He stared at it for at least thirty seconds before registering what it said. An A-minus. Jesus, he'd not only passed this time, he'd kicked some righteous ass!

He grabbed his phone off the table and dialed Marc's number. It rang twice before going to voicemail. He was probably at work. Cole thought about calling back later, but decided to leave a message instead. "Hey, it's me. Hope your day's gone okay. I've got some good news, so give me a call when you get a chance."

He got up to make himself a sandwich, then went back to studying. Next time he looked up, it was closing in on six o'clock. He checked his phone, but there was no return call from Marc. Huh. The diner must've been busy today. His thumb hovered over Marc's number for a few seconds, but then he flicked the phone off and tossed it on the table. This was stupid. He didn't want to come off like some clingy teenager who couldn't go five minutes without talking to his boyfriend.

He finished his assigned reading for the next day, then turned on the TV, clicking channels aimlessly. There was nothing on but sitcom reruns and the news, both equally depressing. Eyelids drooping, he laid down and started to nod off—until a high-pitched whine sounded from down the hall.

Heart racing, he bolted upright. Took him a minute before he realized it was an electric guitar tuning up, not an incoming projectile. Drums joined in a few seconds later, followed by the low thrum of a bass, and then loud, screaming vocals. Christ, they sounded like a cat caught in a fucking lawnmower. This was the kind of shit people listened to now? What happened to Johnny Cash or Springsteen?

Within minutes, his eardrums were on fire and his head was pounding to beat the band. He charged down the hall and banged on their door, but they were playing so damn loud they didn't hear him.

He could go talk to the manager— Except no, he couldn't. The office closed at five, and it was just past seven now. All right, then. He'd go for a walk, give his head a chance to stop throbbing. If they weren't done by the time he got back, he'd kick their fucking door in. He sure as hell wasn't putting up with this for the rest of the night.

It was a bit drizzly out, but Cole zipped up his jacket, jammed his hands in his pockets, and kept walking. His autopilot evidently kicked in, because the next thing he knew, he was standing on the sidewalk outside Marc's apartment. The lights were on inside, casting a pale golden glow through the front curtains, a Thomas-shaped shadow visible on the other side.

Oh, what the hell. What harm would it do to go up and say hello? He wanted to thank Marc for his help with the paper anyway. Without it, he would never have gotten that A-minus.

His pulse sped up as he knocked on Marc's door, heard muffled footsteps on the other side. Saw Marc's surprised expression when the door swung open.

"I wasn't expecting to see you tonight," Marc said.

Well, that was pretty obvious. "Would you believe I just happened to be in the neighborhood?" He chuckled, but Marc didn't join in. Talk about awkward. "Is it okay if I come in for a minute?"

"Um, I'm kind of in the middle of something, but if you want to come back in an hour . . ."

"Hey Marc, I can just leave my stuff here and you can look it over when you've got the time," came a voice from inside. A guy's voice.

Marc glanced in his direction to reply. "You sure? I mean, you've been such a good sport about rescheduling—"

"No, it's fine. I should get going anyway. I need to hit the library tonight before it closes." Then the guy stepped into view. Dark wavy hair, stubbly, cute. Nineteen or twenty. Flannel jacket, messenger bag. Typical Berkeley hipster. Probably pretty close to what Marc had looked like in college.

"Cole, this is my friend Ben. Ben, this is Cole Hammond."

"Good to meet you, man." Ben nodded, scooting past Cole and out the door. "I'll give you a call in a couple days, Marc. Okay?"

"Talk to you then."

Ben's footsteps echoed in the ensuing silence while Cole's heart plummeted to the bottom of the stairs with a big fat thump. He should've known coming here uninvited was a bad idea. At last he said, "I'd better go too. Sorry. I didn't mean to interrupt you both."

"You didn't. Not in the way you mean."

He should've just turned around and left, but for some reason his feet wouldn't move. "Look, I know we didn't promise each other anything, but I didn't think you'd make a date with another guy the day after we—"

"Cole, stop it, okay? Just stop talking and get in here." Marc's mouth tightened as he stepped back to let him inside. "There's a few things we need to get straight."

CHAPTER 10

I poured us coffee, and we sat down at the table. Cole looked at me with this awful, heartbroken expression, like I'd just shot his dog. "I wish you'd told me you already had a boyfriend."

Should've seen that coming a mile away. I sighed and said, "Ben's not my boyfriend. Did you notice we didn't kiss each other goodbye?"

"Then why was he here?"

"Because I invited him." Cole winced at the hard edge in my tone. "Ben's a writer too. We were having a critique session." I smiled to try to knock that look off his face. God, he was such a tender heart, though it'd probably kill him to admit it. Just like every other Marine I'd ever met. "There's nothing going on between me and Ben other than getting our work done. He's not my type, for one thing. For another, he's straight."

Cole stared into his mug. "Sorry I jumped to conclusions. But when you didn't call me back . . ."

"I was planning to as soon as Ben left. It was crazy at the diner today. I didn't even listen to your message until after I got home. And frankly, I thought we could do with a little space after four days together."

He tensed. "Is that your way of telling me you didn't have a good time?"

Oh, Cole. Such a typical guy—completely fucking clueless. "You know I did. But that doesn't mean you get to tell me who I can and can't socialize with. Sure, I'd like to see where this relationship goes, but I have friends. I have a job. Two jobs, really—the diner and writing. If we're going to go on seeing each other, you need to understand there are parts of my life you won't necessarily be involved in. I mean, you don't expect me to tag along with you to class every day, do you?"

He took his time thinking about it before nodding. "You're right. I get it. Stop being such a control freak."

"Just try to cool it, that's all I ask. I know it's hardwired into your brain, so I'm not expecting miracles." I got up to give him a kiss. "And now, don't take this the wrong way, but I'm kicking you out. I didn't get any writing done over the weekend, so I really need to crank on it. I promised my editor I'd have my new book on her desk by this Friday. Which means I probably won't see you again until next weekend."

Cole gave a resigned nod and stood, wrapping his arms around me. "Is it all right if I call you tomorrow?"

"Sure. You can even drop by the diner if you want. But don't get bent out of shape if I'm too busy to talk, okay?"

"Well, finishing a new book should be cause for celebration, right?" He grinned as I walked him to the door. "I'll try to dream up something special to do. Other than plundering that sweet ass of yours again."

Thoughts of all the times he'd done it this past weekend flitted through my brain and sent half the blood in my body racing southward. Better get him out of here before I caved and lost any hope of writing for the rest of the night.

"Take care," I murmured, giving him a last kiss before sending him on his way.

I stood at the top of the stairs watching until he reached the corner, crossed the street, and moved out of eyeshot. Part of me ached to call him back, while that other, annoyingly sane part screamed, "Are you *crazy?*" One long weekend didn't mean we'd be together forever. Letting him work his way under my skin so soon was ill-advised, to put it mildly.

God, sometimes behaving like a grownup really sucked.

Cole picked me up at my place Saturday night in a battered black Jeep Grand Cherokee with a Marine Corps bumper sticker peeling off its rear window. My eyes bugged out the moment I saw it. "You have a *car?* And you didn't bother to mention it?"

Cole shrugged. "I don't drive it that much. It's easier to get around town on foot or the bus." He opened the passenger-side door for me. "Besides, how do you think I got here from North Carolina?"

"There are these things called airplanes."

"No thanks. I hate flying. I must've racked up half a million miles in personnel transports over the last twelve years." He shut my door, then swung around to the driver's side, climbed in and switched on the ignition. "Folsom Prison Blues" blared forth from the CD player. He punched the off button, flashing me a sheepish smile. "Sorry about that."

I smiled too. "Go ahead and turn it back on if you want. I like Johnny. Just not at ninety decibels."

"Okay." On went the music at a much lower volume, and then he pulled away from the curb and drove down to Ashby, eventually swinging onto southbound 580. "So you finished your book on time, huh?"

"Just barely. Had to pull a couple of all nighters." As if on cue, I stifled a yawn. "It's nice having a whole weekend without a project hanging over my head for a change."

"You planning to start something new right away?"

"I'll probably take a few days off. Any longer than that and I get antsy. I always feel like a slacker when I'm not working on something. I had four books out last year. This year I wrote six."

Cole whistled. I peered out the rain-spattered windshield as we approached the Bay Bridge toll plaza. "Where are we going?"

"I told you, it's a surprise."

I groaned inwardly. Why was he being so coy when it was obvious we were headed into the city? "C'mon, give me a hint."

"Now who's being a control freak?" Cole inched up to the booth to pay the toll, then sailed onto the bridge. San Francisco's skyline flickered up at us through the fog like a thousand candles. "All right, let's just say you're about to visit one of your favorite old neighborhoods, and I'm about to visit it for the first time."

Ah. "You've lived here since August and you've never been to the Castro?" Then again, I probably shouldn't have been surprised that a guy shy about holding hands with me in public hadn't explored San Francisco's most famous gay district.

"Nope." He grinned. "Guess I was waiting for the right person to show me the sights."

"I wish you'd told me before. We could've come over on a weeknight. It's a fucking madhouse on Fridays and Saturdays. All the bars and clubs have lines down the block."

"Then we can just walk around for a while. That's fun too, isn't it?"

"If we can snag a parking place."

Of course we couldn't find a damn thing on the street. After driving around for forty-five minutes, Cole finally pulled into a pay-through-the-nose private lot. This time, when I handed him a few bucks to help cover it, I wouldn't take no for an answer.

I'd hoped the damp weather might've thinned the crowds out a bit, but the main drag—no pun intended—was still pretty packed. We pulled up the hoods of our jackets and walked the gauntlet, ambling past bars, cafés, and cheesy gift shops. Some of the signage had changed over the past few years, but the demographic had remained the same.

Cole craned his neck trying to take everything in, completely unaware that he himself was turning heads. I could've sworn two or three guys literally froze in their tracks staring at him. I longed to tell them all to eat their hearts out, but instead I just grinned and grabbed his hand.

Surprisingly, tonight he wasn't the least bit self-conscious about it. In fact, his fingers closed over mine in a death grip, squeezing so hard I had to make him let go. When I saw how pale he was, sweat beaded on his forehead and upper lip, every alarm bell in my head went off. I tucked my arm through his and tugged him under a deserted bus stop shelter. "You okay?"

"Yeah," Cole breathed. "There's just a lot of people out there. It's kind of overwhelming."

"Maybe we should go."

He bit his lip. "But we only got here a little while ago."

"You don't need to stay on my account," I said gently. "I've been here dozens of times."

"I'll be okay," he said, rubbing a hand over his face. "One more hour, all right? Otherwise the drive was hardly worth it."

Against my better judgment, I nodded and offered him my hand again. "Okay. But stay close."

We started walking again, and quickly spied a funky little hole-in-the-wall bar on a side street. Cole tried to drag me inside, but I hung back.

"C'mon, Marc, just one beer and we'll go. I can't visit the Castro for the first time and not have a drink." He opened the door, squinting into the half-darkness. "Doesn't look too busy."

Not compared to the joints closer to Castro Street, but most of the seats were still occupied. A protest floated to my lips, but quickly died there. It was only one drink. What could it hurt?

It was actually a cute place once my eyes adjusted to the dim lighting. No more than twenty tables, with a hilariously kitschy Polynesian tiki theme. Cole went up to order our drinks from one of the bare-chested bartenders in leis and loud Hawaiian shorts, while I snagged a relatively quiet corner table.

"Isn't it a trip?" he said once he returned with our beers, the buzz of surrounding voices prompting him to lean across the table so I could hear him. "There sure as hell isn't anyplace like this in North Carolina."

"You didn't know how lucky you were, huh?"

He shot me a puzzled look. "What, you don't like it?"

"The bar scene gets old pretty fast. I mean, sure, it's fun at first, but you don't meet a lot of quality people. I got tired of fucking guys I couldn't remember half an hour later."

"Yeah, me too." At my raised eyebrows, he added, "I've been in gay bars before, Marc. Where do you think I picked up guys for my . . . previous encounters?" He glanced around at all the other chatting, flirting patrons. "But you're right. It is pretty empty and pointless. Guess I just got distracted by the new shiny."

"And it's fine to get distracted. I went a little crazy when I first moved to the Bay Area. Out drinking and partying on the weekends, waking up in other guys' beds. It's something every gay man has to get out of his system." I paused, the next few words hanging on the edge of my tongue. At last I just blurted, "So if you want to, I think you should."

He burst out laughing, but when he realized I wasn't joking, he slowly set down his beer. "You're giving me a pass to *cheat* on you?"

"Look, everyone's tempted to experiment when they first come out. You're like a kid at Christmas, and you just want to raid the toy store and play with everything *right now*. I did all that before I was twenty years old. Now's your chance. I don't want to hold you back."

"You're not." He reached for my hand, curling his fingers tightly around mine. "Believe me, I've had enough meaningless fucks in my life to know I don't want any more. I'm ready to take it to the next level. So . . ." Leaning closer, he whispered into my ear, "Are we together, or aren't we?"

I'd been waiting for this ever since last weekend, and dreading it too. As long as the words remained unsaid, there was no real risk—at least, that's what I told myself. But I'd just given him an out and he'd turned it down. Maybe he really did want to be with me as much as I wanted to be with him.

Or maybe he had no idea what he really wanted. Just like Tony. Better to hold him at arm's length than let myself fall hard for one more guy who'd disappear once the thrill was gone. But maybe this time it wouldn't happen. Maybe Cole was the real deal.

Maybe.

"We've known each other barely two weeks," I said. "How can you be so sure it'll work?"

His eyebrows arched. "What, you're asking for a guarantee? There isn't anyone in the whole fucking world who can give you that. All I know is, you're the only guy I've ever spent the night with who I actually wanted to wake up with the next morning. I like talking to you. I like having dinner with you. I've had more fun with you in the last couple weeks than I've had with anyone else in the past twelve years. I don't want it to end."

"Neither do I," I admitted at last, all the air sailing from my lungs when Cole flung his big, strong arms around me. Black spots dancing before my eyes, I reluctantly pushed him away. "Not that I'm complaining, but what happened to your phobia about public displays of affection?"

"If people want to stare at us, let 'em. I'm too happy to give a fuck." He flashed me the world's silliest grin before leaning in to kiss me. God, how my heart thumped with joy at that.

We finished our beers and headed out into the chilly, drizzly December evening. About a block from the parking lot, a sharp crack split the air. Then another, and another after that. For one horrible, panicked moment, I thought they were gunshots, until I saw the ancient VW bug backfiring across the street. Then I realized Cole had let go of my hand. He wasn't even standing next to me anymore.

I quickly scanned both sides of the street, but couldn't see him amid the bustling Friday night crowd. My heart sped and a cold fist tightened around my windpipe, until I forced myself to calm down and *think.* Where the hell could he have disappeared to?

Elbowing my way through a cluster of laughing, wobbly-drunk guys on a nearby corner, I started checking side streets. "Cole! *Cole!* Where the fuck *are* you?" I screamed myself hoarse, scouring every doorway, fire escape, and public restroom I could find. No sign of him anywhere.

Maybe he'd tried to call me, and I simply hadn't heard in the roar of the crowd. Fingers trembling, I yanked my phone from my pocket and checked the missed calls. Nothing. I tried calling him, but it just rang and rang, then went to voicemail.

Maybe he'd gone back the way we came. I turned around and headed north for a couple of blocks. The crowd up here had thinned out, the noise level dropping to the point where I could hear the frantic beat of my own pulse echoing between my ears. I tried Cole's number again, and stopped dead at a faint chirping noise.

I followed it down the next alley, where I caught a glimpse of a familiar gray rain slicker and the toe of a white sneaker peeking out from behind a dumpster. My knees nearly buckled when I found him huddled there, gripping the edge of the dumpster so hard the skin over his knuckles looked ready to split. Taking cover, the way any Marine would in a combat situation. Just like that night at his apartment.

The alley reeked of piss and rotting garbage, but I didn't give a fuck. I dropped to my knees beside him and murmured,

"Cole, it's me. I'm going to put my hand on your shoulder now, okay?"

I don't know whether he heard me or not, but at least he didn't stop me. Didn't freak out even further and try to attack me, the way Rob had that one time. Still, he trembled like a frightened child, panting and drenched in sweat.

"Look at me, Cole." I waited, breath stopping in my lungs as he slowly turned his head in my direction, his wide-eyed, petrified expression fading. "You remember me now? Remember where we are?"

He sagged against me, buried his face in my shoulder as a ragged sob caught in his throat. "Jesus, Marc, I'm sorry. I didn't mean—"

Now he sounded more humiliated than scared. I tightened my arms around him and pressed a gentle kiss to his temple. "C'mon, let's get you home."

Cole didn't want to give up the keys to the Jeep, but I refused to get in until he handed them to me. We rode along in silence, Cole staring blankly out the window.

He gave me a sad, resigned look as we pulled up in front of my place. "Thanks for driving," he said. "I can take it from here."

I shook my head. "Don't be silly. You're coming upstairs."

"You sure you still want to be with a head case like me?"

"Stop it. You're not a head case. You're a guy who's been through a hell of a lot." I leaned in to kiss him, my thumb skimming over his cheek. "Look, I'm not about to let you go home alone after what just happened. So c'mon. We can talk about it some more once we get inside."

Thomas greeted us at the door, meowing and begging for

kibble. I shooed him away, then helped Cole out of his jacket and pointed him toward the bathroom. "Go take a nice hot shower. I'll wait for you in bed."

I gave Thomas a little food so he wouldn't bother us, then grabbed a bottle of water to soothe my sore throat, cued up some Miles Davis on my laptop, got undressed, and crawled under the covers. Cole padded in naked a few minutes later and crumpled onto the mattress, one arm flung over his eyes.

"I'm so, so sorry," he murmured. "I don't know what the fuck happened."

"It was that car backfiring. Sent you right back to Iraq, didn't it?"

"Yeah, I guess. How'd you know what to do?

I brushed my fingertips through the short damp hair on top of his head. "Rob was in Somalia during the Battle of Mogadishu in '93. It haunted him even years later, after I met him."

Cole said nothing. I nudged him until he let me slip my arm around his waist. Finally he looked at me. "So why haven't you sought treatment?"

"Because the Corps cut off my benefits when they kicked me out, and who the hell can afford private insurance?"

"Then go to campus health services. They have therapists there. If they can't help you, they'll refer you to someone who can. It's all covered by your tuition."

"I know that. I read the fucking pamphlet when I enrolled."

"Then why haven't you taken advantage of it? Do you want to keep on having these flashbacks for—"

He jerked upright and turned his back to me. "I don't need to talk to anybody. I need 'em to refill my fucking Xanax."

Just when I'd started thinking he wasn't a typical Marine, there he went acting all macho and bull-headed as the rest of them. "Post-traumatic stress is nothing to mess with, Cole. You should talk to a professional."

"How the hell can I talk about some of the shit I've seen? No civilian therapist could ever understand. I held my best friend in my arms while he died, his guts spilling all over the ground. And at my separation hearing, they tried to make it sound like we were—" He hugged his knees to his chest. "He was my friend, not my lover. We were like brothers. I was best man at his wedding. He knew about me, and he kept my secret. And I tried to save him, tried to get him to hold on until the medics got to us, but I didn't . . . I couldn't . . ."

A minute ago I'd been royally pissed at him, but now all I wanted was to hold him and tell him everything would be okay. Even if I couldn't imagine how.

I woke up around one in the morning with Cole snoring softly into my shoulder. He looked so adorable asleep, his lips parted slightly, all the stress lines around his eyes and mouth gone. I lay there staring at the ceiling for about half an hour before I realized I wasn't sleepy anymore. So I gave Cole a gentle push to get him to roll over, then threw on my robe, grabbed my laptop, and took it into the kitchen.

Like I'd told Cole, I hadn't planned to get going on a new project right away, but for some reason I felt compelled to start typing. The words swirled around in my brain, pouring out faster than my fingers could keep up. It was more like journaling than creative writing, a chronicle of everything Cole and I had done together over the past couple weeks. A diary of our relationship, and my thoughts about it.

I worked away for a while until I heard a muffled grunt from the other room, followed by the soft rustle of bedcovers and a sleep-slurred, "Marc? Where'd you go?"

I padded back into the bedroom, Cole's arms looping around my waist the moment I crawled back into bed. "I don't like waking up with you gone," he said. "What were you doing?"

"Oh, just fooling around with some new ideas. No big deal." Cole inched closer, and something very stiff and insistent prodded my belly. "Speaking of big, why don't I give you a little help with that?" I was just about to duck under the comforter to do so when I thought of something he might like even better. "Have you ever bottomed?"

He did a startled—but not an unpleasantly startled—double-take. "Um, no. Never."

"Really? You mean you haven't heard that old saying, 'A real Marine holds his own legs up when you fuck him'?"

If he hadn't been lying down, he would've fallen over laughing. "Somehow I missed that one. Must be a big hit with the enlisted guys, though."

Oh, he had no idea. "Have you ever *wanted* to bottom?"

"Well, sure, I'm curious about it, but doesn't it hurt?"

"After all the times I've come with your cock inside me, you really have to ask?" Now we both laughed. "Seriously, it can hurt a bit at first. But with a lot of lube and careful prep, it feels wonderful. Rob was a total top until the first time we decided to switch off. He liked getting fucked so much he never wanted to climb in the driver's seat again."

"So you're that good, huh?"

I gave him an "Oh, knock it off!" look. "If you don't try it at least once, you're missing out."

"I'm definitely not against it, but . . ." His forehead went all crinkly. "I'm not sure I'm ready yet."

"Why don't I give you a taste?" I reached over to grab the bottle of baby oil I kept on the bedside table. "We'll go slow, take our time. I'll make sure it feels good. Okay?"

"Okay." He rolled onto his back with a smile. "You're the boss."

He spread his legs wide, obviously expecting me to make

an immediate dive for his ass, but I had other plans first. His nipples stood up in the semi-cool air like little thumbs, begging for the edge of my teeth. I took each of them in my mouth in turn as Cole gasped and writhed under me, his hand twisting in my hair to urge me on.

Didn't take long before his cock was bobbing against his belly like a neglected flagpole. I poured some baby oil into my hands, rubbed them together, and slowly smoothed them over Cole's cock and balls.

"That's . . . that feels really nice."

"Don't you ever use oil when you jerk off?" I asked.

"Not for a long time, but, *wow*, your hands feel good. So soft and strong."

"I thought you'd like it." I liked it too. I liked the feel of his cock pulsing warm and heavy in my hand, the glide of the smooth, shiny skin there. I *really* liked the sounds he made: sweet, desperate little gasps and moans as his fingers scrabbled at the covers. All because of *me* and the pleasure I was giving him. Talk about a power trip.

His face had gone bright pink by the time I started jacking him in earnest. He panted, mouth falling open, sweat pouring off him as if he'd just run a marathon. God, he looked so tempting and delicious, I couldn't resist; I leaned in and licked a long, leisurely stripe up his throat, tasting his skin, salt and the faint tang of shower soap tingling on my tongue.

"Oh God, oh Jesus, oh fucking Christ I'm gonna—"

No he wasn't, not if my fingers gripping the base of his dick had anything to say about it. Orgasm averted for the moment, I traced a pair of slippery digits along his perineum, my index finger circling his hole, easing in up to the first knuckle. Damn, but he was tight. I tried to go in deeper, but he gave a tiny grunt and shook his head. Time for more oil.

At last I got one finger inside him, but the tight, strained expression on his face told me he wasn't enjoying it. "Do you want to stop?" I asked, stroking his thigh with my free hand.

"No, it's okay. I mean, it felt fine up until you started doing *that*."

"You need to relax. Stop fighting it. If you tense up, of course it's going to hurt." After gently extricating my other hand, I bent down to rub my cheek against his belly, following with a soft kiss, his springy happy trail tickling my lips. When I swirled the tip of my tongue around and then into his navel, he shuddered and let out a pleasantly startled chuckle. "Close your eyes and breathe," I whispered. "Let all your tension out on the exhale."

I put my hand on his chest to guide him through it, the two of us breathing in unison. Quietly, amazingly intimate. I traced my fingers over his skin from shoulder to waist, grinning as he let out these wonderful little moans and his cock began to stir again.

This time, my freshly-lubed finger glided right inside him, so I pulled out and pushed back in, adding a second. "How's that feel?"

"Good," he breathed. "I mean, a little weird, but good." He glanced up at me with that hot glow in his eyes I absolutely adored, and licked his lips. "Is that how my cock feels when I'm in you?"

"Actually, it feels more like this." I started moving slowly, fucking him with my hand. Soon he thrust back, giving as good as he got. I leaned down to give him what he'd wanted earlier, the crown of his cock gliding between my lips, baby oil and salty-bitter pre-cum exploding hot and slick over my tongue. I could've kept this up all night, listening to his yelps and gasps.

He buried his fingers in my hair, clutching at me like a drowning man as he shot down my throat with a spent, shattered groan.

"Jesus," he huffed, trying to catch his breath, "You weren't kidding when you said I was missing out." He tugged me down for a kiss, stroking my damp cheek. "But you didn't—"

"S'okay. Tonight was all yours."

"You sure?"

I smiled and kissed him back. "Don't worry about me, I'm fine."

My cock hung heavily between my thighs, still half-hard, yet I had no real desire to get off. Seeing Cole satisfied was more than enough to content me. Maybe I couldn't completely erase the terrible burden of pain and guilt he carried around with him every damn day, but at least I could help him forget about it for a while. And maybe, in time, I could even help him heal.

CHAPTER 11

"So what're your plans for the holidays?" I asked when Cole came by the diner to have supper with me. "Christmas is in two weeks, and you haven't said a word about it. When are you leaving to go visit your folks?"

Cole swallowed his mouthful of cheeseburger. "I'm not."

"What?" I set down my fork. "Don't tell me they didn't invite you."

"Mama did, but I told her I had other plans. My dad hasn't come to the phone to talk to me once in all the time I've been here. Can't imagine seeing him face to face would be any more pleasant."

"Well, that's just . . ." Sad? Tragic? A crying shame? All of the above? I sighed, then took another bite of my salad. "Sorry. I wish things were different."

"So do I, but there's no point crying about it. It is what it is."

Back in stoic Marine mode, just like every other time I'd tried to talk to him about his family.

"You're welcome to come down to San Diego with me," I said finally. "My mom would love to meet you. She's already told me how proud she is that I'm dating an officer."

"Ex-officer."

"Once a Marine, always a Marine, right?"

"Depends who you ask." He finished his burger, then started nibbling listlessly at his fries. "Thanks for the offer, but I think I'll stay here in town. Get a head start on my reading for next semester."

"You're going to spend Christmas *studying?*"

He shrugged. "It's just another day when you're by yourself."

A sharp pang of guilt pricked at me, though I was sure he didn't mean it that way. He'd learned his lesson about playing the passive-aggressive card the night he'd shown up at my door uninvited. Still, the thought of him spending Christmas alone in that crappy, cramped apartment of his bummed me out.

"I'd stay home with you, except I haven't seen Mom since last Easter. She'd be disappointed if I canceled. And frankly, so would I."

"I don't want you to cancel. Don't worry about me. I'll still be here when you get home." He smiled and knocked back his last sip of coffee. "It's nice knowing someone who actually looks forward to seeing his family. I love my dad, but we've always had a contentious relationship. 'Two bulls butting heads,' that's what Mama calls us. He gave me such shit when I applied to the Academy. Said I was spitting in the face of family tradition; I come from a long line of non-commissioned officers. But the day I got my appointment letter, he was pretty damn proud."

I blinked, my shoulders stiffening. "Is that why you don't want to come with me? Because Camp Pendleton's nearby?"

He hesitated before giving a grudging nod. "I'd rather not look at all those guys walking around town wearing a uniform I wish I was still wearing."

Now I knew what getting punched in the heart felt like. Took me a moment to recover. "If it's any consolation, once we get to Mom's, we'll probably stay put. I've only got Thursday through Sunday off, and Christmas is on Friday."

"You're flying on Christmas Eve?" Cole's eyes widened. "Jesus. And you called *me* a masochist."

"It's the only way I can get there and back in time."

"Screw that. I'll come with you, provided you let me drive."

I stared at him. "You're serious?"

"Somebody's got to make sure you arrive safely."

"Oh, and you indulging your control freak tendencies has nothing to do with it, huh?" I got up to clear our plates, indulging my own impulse to give him a kiss on the cheek. "Well, okay. This time I'll let it slide."

He walked me home and kissed me goodnight on my doorstep. When I invited him in, he shook his head. "Better not. I need to get to the library tonight and study."

That explained the backpack. He didn't normally bring it along on our dinner dates. "Just think, the semester will be over soon and you'll have two glorious weeks off."

"Not from my new neighbors, I won't. This thrash-metal band moved in across the hall last week. I've just about gone deaf from all their fucking practicing."

That explained the purplish circles under his eyes. I'd chalked them up to a few all-nighters. "Haven't you complained to the management?"

"Sure I have, and believe me, I'm not the only one. But the regulations are pretty clear—they can play as loud as they want 'til ten o'clock." He sighed. "Makes me wish I was back in the barracks."

"Since when were you ever *in* the barracks, *Major* Hammond?" I unlocked the door, grabbed his jacket sleeve and yanked him inside. "Feel free to come here to study anytime you want, even when I'm at home. But if I'm writing, I need you to leave me alone until I'm done, okay?"

He stared at me for a moment as if he expected me to say I was kidding. "Okay. Thanks. I appreciate it."

"No problem. I don't know why you didn't mention it before."

"Because I didn't want you to feel obligated to go out of your way for me."

"It's not going out of my way. This is what significant others do for each other, you know." Except he didn't know. This was all new territory for him. I gave him a quick kiss, then stepped toward the living room. "I'm going to go work for a couple hours. The kitchen table's all yours."

As usual lately, the time flew by. I cranked out six fairly good pages, saved the file, and shut down my laptop. Cole was still studying, so I padded into the kitchen as quietly as possible to avoid disturbing him. He looked comfortable, slouched back in his chair, absorbed in his reading. As if he'd always been there. My gaze dropped to the floor, and there was Thomas, curled up on Cole's feet like a big, furry donut. I couldn't help laughing.

"I get the feeling he doesn't want me to leave," Cole said, bending down to give his ears a scritch.

That made two of us.

Chapter 12

Cole picked Marc up at the diner when he got off work the Wednesday before Christmas. "Four days away from this place! I can't fucking believe it," Marc said, tossing his bag in the back of the Jeep before climbing into the passenger seat. "The last couple hours were dead like a dead thing. Terry almost drove me insane drumming her nails on the counter." Grinning, Marc leaned in to give him a kiss. Cole's heart tripped double-time whenever he did that—and damn if wasn't the best feeling ever. "How about you? Get everything finished?"

"Yup. Emailed my last paper around noon. Now I'm free as a bird." He grinned back. "Or rather, we both are."

"Damn right. Let's get out of here."

The pre-holiday traffic was pretty hairy leaving the Bay Area, but things eased up once they reached the southbound Highway 5 interchange. Cole turned on some music. "One good thing about this stretch of road—it's a straight shot."

Marc nodded, staring out the window at the wide, flat expanse of asphalt and farmland surrounding them, peppered with taillights and the occasional overpass and mileage signs. "Highway 101's a more scenic drive, though," Marc said. "Might be nice if we could come back that way."

"Sure, why not?" It started raining, so Cole switched on the windshield wipers. "Hope you told your mom not to wait up for us. We'll probably get in pretty late. Or early, depending on how you look at it."

"That's fine. She said we should let ourselves in. She's got the extra bedroom all ready."

"*One* bedroom? Um, maybe I should sleep on the couch."

"Oh, fuck that. I'm not spending our first Christmas in separate beds. Mom's a big girl. She knows we're Doing It." God, he even used air quotes. Cole had to stifle a snicker. "Seriously, though, Rob used to stay over with me at Mom's all the time. She was fine with it."

"She must be one open-minded lady. That kind of thing would never fly in my parents' house."

"Mom's always been a free spirit. She left home at seventeen and she's made her own way ever since. No apologies, no regrets."

They drove along silently for another few miles, until the CD they were listening to ended. Cole switched out Johnny Cash for the Eagles and began tapping his palms on the wheel to "Hotel California," a question he'd been pondering awhile whirling in his mind. If he was ever going to ask, now seemed the best time. "How come you've never mentioned your father?"

"There's nothing to mention. I've never met him."

Marc stated it in such a matter of fact way that Cole almost didn't believe him at first. How could he act like it was no big deal? "But you know who he is?"

"Oh, yeah. Mom had a picture she showed me when I got old enough to start asking about him. I look a little bit like him around the eyes and mouth, and I ended up with his dark hair. But he wasn't interested in being a dad. Mom said he couldn't get his ass transferred fast enough once she told him she was pregnant."

"He was a Marine?"

Marc gave him that cute, crooked smile Cole adored so much. "Evidently, being a tag chaser runs in the family. And before you ask—no, I'm not attracted to Marines because I'm looking for a father figure. I mean, Rob and Tony were both a few years older, but it's never been about me trying to find something I lacked as a child. I had a great childhood. Mom and I did just fine on our own."

"Okay, I believe you. But since you brought it up . . ."

"I like masculine guys, and Marines are about as masculine as you can get. I used to get excited just watching them walk down the street. The first guy I ever fucked was a Marine. I met him in a coffeehouse in Oceanside, and he took me to a motel. I thought he'd kick me out on my ass when I told him I'd never done anything before, but he was actually pretty nice. Gentle. He took his time, made sure everything felt good. Then he made me come so hard I almost passed out. That was it for me. I was hooked."

Cole let loose a long, slow hiss of a breath. Imagining Marc giving it up for the first time made his hands strangle the wheel and his pulse rate spiral, the crotch of his jeans rapidly growing a size too small. Jesus. Perfect time for a raging hard-on—hurtling down a highway in the middle of fucking nowhere.

Eyes glued to the road, he did logarithms in his head until it subsided. He finally glanced over at Marc to discover he'd dozed off. Well, no wonder. Between the diner and his writing, he worked too damn hard. And now Marc had shouldered the added responsibility of looking after him. Cole still had no idea what he'd done to deserve such devotion, but he sure as hell wasn't about to take it for granted. Smiling, he gave Marc's shoulder a quick squeeze, then turned down the music and kept driving.

We arrived at Mom's condo at oh-dark-thirty, so worn out after nine hours on the road that all we could do was stumble blindly through the front door and down the hall to the guest bedroom. Cole would've fallen into bed fully clothed if I hadn't grabbed him by the belt loops, unzipped him, and skinned down his jeans and boxers. He managed to tug off his t-shirt, kiss me, and mumble "G'night" before landing face-first on the nearest pillow. I shucked my own clothes and crawled in beside him. Despite my nap in the car earlier, I was already half-unconscious by the time I heard him start to snore.

I jerked awake a couple hours later to find Cole perched on the edge of the bed, shaking hard enough to make the bed frame squeak. "Hey," I whispered, sliding my hand gently onto his arm, "I'm right here. C'mon back, okay?"

"Jesus." He flopped down next to me and dragged a hand over his face. "Sorry. Forgot where I was for a minute."

"It's all right. You're safe." I slung my arm around his waist and laid my head on his sweat-damp chest. His heart was pounding like a fucking gong, but after a few minutes, it started to slow down. "Better now?"

"A little." Sighing, he tangled his fingers in my hair. "And I was hoping to get through this trip without any freak-outs. No such fucking luck."

I bit my lip. "You could do something about it, you know."

Another sigh, more exasperated than exhausted. "Drop it, okay? I don't want to talk about it right now."

"You never want to talk about it. That's the problem."

"No," he snapped, pulling away, "the problem is you don't know when to let things go. It's bad enough having these fucking nightmares without you nagging me about 'em all the time."

I flopped onto my back. *Shit.* I knew I should've waited until we got home to bring this up again. Well, no point in clamming up now that he was already pissed at me. "This isn't some kind of endurance test. You're not gonna score points for being all stoic and macho."

He rolled over to face away from me, shrugging me off when I tried to touch his arm. "Leave me the fuck alone."

Chapter 13

Cole woke up alone to sunshine pouring through the bedroom curtains and the tantalizing aroma of fresh coffee tickling his nostrils. A thermal mug sat on the bedside table with a yellow Post-It attached, "We're in the kitchen" scribbled in Marc's sloppy handwriting.

Cole scooped up the mug, popped the lid, and swirled it, taking a long, luxurious sip. It was good coffee. French roast, strong and hot, just the way he liked it—although after last night, he was amazed Marc hadn't left him a lump of coal instead. Time to swallow his pride and apologize.

He threw on his jeans and a clean t-shirt, grabbed his shaving kit, and padded down the hall to the bathroom. A queasy fluttering in his stomach surged as he climbed in the shower, and not just because of last night. What was he so worried about? It was Marc's mom, after all. If she was anything like him, Cole knew he'd love her. But would she love him, or would she take one look at him and see the guy who'd dumped her thirty years ago? Or even worse, would she see the two guys who'd dumped Marc?

But the gentle, throaty voice floating from down the hall didn't sound like a woman who'd hate another person on sight. At least, that's what Cole hoped. He held on to that hope as he toweled dry, dressed, pasted on a smile, and stepped into the kitchen. Marc and his mother sat at the table in their robes, nursing their respective mugs of tea and coffee while they did a newspaper crossword puzzle together. In *ink*.

"'Morning," Cole said, shooting Marc a nervous glance. It seemed like Marc's mom picked up on it, but she had the good grace to avert her eyes for a moment. "Didn't mean to oversleep."

"You're allowed to oversleep when you're on vacation," Marc's mother replied, gesturing toward the empty chair across from her as she stood. Cole had to admit she was a striking woman. Considering Marc's age, he figured she had to be at least fifty, though her clear, smooth skin made her look younger. She shared Marc's slender build and green eyes, but with natural-looking auburn curls instead of Marc's dark ones, shot through with a few strands of gray. "Sit down and I'll get you some more coffee."

"Oh, that's not necessary, ma'am. I'm perfectly capable of getting it myself."

She broke out in a wide, toothy smile, poking Marc in the shoulder. "You weren't kidding when you said he was a gentleman. However," she went on, glancing back at Cole, "guests don't wait on themselves in my house. Have a seat, Cole."

He couldn't very well protest now without sounding impolite, so he pulled out the chair and sat down. Marc gave him a tiny smile, his hand sliding across the table to clasp Cole's fingers.

"Does this mean I'm forgiven for acting like such a jerk last night?" Cole asked under his breath.

"As if you have to ask. Why don't we relax and enjoy our visit, okay?" Leaning in close, Marc studied him with raised eyebrows before taking a cautious sniff. "You've already showered and shaved?"

"Well, I wasn't about to meet your mama looking like a *complete* slob."

Marc's mouth twitched the way it did when he was about to burst out laughing, but he stifled it with a long sip from his mug as his mother came back with Cole's fresh cup. "Thank you, ma'am," Cole said, taking it from her. "It's good coffee."

"Well, thank *you*. And it's Melinda, by the way. While I appreciate your lovely manners, whenever someone calls me ma'am, it makes me feel like my own mother. I may be old, but I'm not *that* old yet. Although this one's certainly aged me a few years." She shot Marc a pointed look before turning back to Cole. "Marc tells me you're in law school, but you're not enjoying it very much."

"I don't think you're supposed to enjoy it, but . . ." He shrugged. "It's a rough adjustment. I've been out of school a long time."

"I considered going to law school," she said, sipping at her coffee. "I was a legal secretary for over twenty years."

"What made you change your mind?"

"I came pretty close. I'd already started studying for the LSAT before I realized I didn't want to become one of those arrogant jerks I had to work with every day. So I became a different kind of arrogant jerk and went for my MBA instead."

"Tell him what you do now," Marc prompted.

"What, so Cole can join in while you laugh at me?" She rolled her eyes. "Oh, all right. I'm the marketing director at Legoland."

Cole stared at them both in turn. "*Legos*? Those plastic blocks kids build stuff out of?"

"Yup. They've got these huge Lego dioramas, and rides, and a water park," Marc said. "The place is packed during the summer. It's really not as lame as it sounds."

"Oh, thank you for that, spawn of mine. Remind me to smack you the next time I get up."

All three of them laughed, and Cole felt something inside him unclench. She didn't hate him. In fact, she seemed to like him, and he certainly liked her.

"Hang in there, Cole," Melinda went on. "I hadn't seen the inside of a classroom in two decades when I went back, and let me tell you, it was brutal. All my classmates were young enough to be my kids. They ran rings around me. I spent most of the first year feeling like a big failure, struggling to hold down my job and take classes at night. I wanted to throw in the towel every week, but I'm glad I didn't. If I had, I'd still be living in that crappy apartment in Vista where I raised Marc."

"At least Vista's not as run down as Oceanside," Marc interjected. "Growing up there wasn't that bad."

"I still wish I could've done better. Though you turned out pretty well despite all my mistakes." She drained her mug, then stood. "I should get dressed and drag myself to the grocery store before it turns into too big of a madhouse. We're on our own this year, I'm afraid. Marc's aunt and uncle decided to stay put up in Tahoe, which is just as well, considering all the snow they're getting. Marc, make Cole and yourself some breakfast. There's eggs, sausage, and juice in the fridge."

No sooner had she left the kitchen than Cole realized, "I should've offered to go to the store for her."

"She'll be fine. She's gone grocery shopping every Christmas Eve for as long as I can remember." Marc got up and started rummaging in the fridge. "There's onions, tomatoes, and mushrooms in here too. You want an omelet?"

"Isn't there anything else I can do? I feel useless just sitting around being waited on."

"Why do I get the feeling holidays at your house were pretty tense even before you came out?"

Cole thought back to all those evenings with his father glaring at him across the table. "Family dinners any day of the week weren't a hell of a lot better."

"Well, you know why it's called a vacation? Because you *don't work*." Marc came and sat back down, reaching for his hand. "Will you please *relax?* This is supposed to be a fun trip, and you're already stressing me out. The TV's in the living room. Why don't you go watch the game or something?"

"There's no football 'til tomorrow."

"Then read the newspaper, or go get my laptop and surf the 'net for a while. It's Christmas. Consider this my gift to you—two whole days of being a lazy lump on the couch." Marc kissed him softly, then stood. "Now go on."

Cole was halfway to the living room before Marc's mention of gifts made him realize: "Shit! I didn't get you or your mom anything."

Marc appeared in the doorway, tying on a red apron with roosters on it. "Mom and I haven't exchanged gifts since I graduated high school. My visits are enough of a gift for both of us."

"But my mama would kill me if she knew I didn't bring something for the lady of the house. It's expected back home."

"You're not back home, okay? Mom and I don't expect anything except for you to enjoy yourself." He ambled over and laid his hands on Cole's shoulders, pulling him close. "Guess how many other guys I've brought home to meet her since I've lived in Berkeley?"

"I don't know. A couple?"

"Try none."

Was he *serious*?

Marc wagged his head. "I keep telling you how special you are, but you don't want to believe it. I mean, what's it going to take? Do I have to get down on my knees?" He smiled. "Not that I mind, but we'd better wait 'til Mom leaves."

"Okay, okay, I get it," Cole said. "I'll go relax. Or try to, anyway."

"Good. I'll call you when breakfast is ready."

Hands in his pockets, Cole strolled into the living room, immediately struck by the tall, white-flocked tree with blue and silver ornaments standing in the far corner by the fireplace. Just like Marc said, there were no gifts under it. It was a nice room, warm and inviting, with a long leather couch, a pair of matching armchairs, and colorful Navajo-print throw rugs. Spacious, too—he could've fit his entire apartment in here.

He dropped onto the couch, let his head loll back on the cushions, and shut his eyes, calmness washing over him at last. After just a few minutes, he felt more at home here than he ever had in the succession of nondescript houses on various bases where he'd grown up. Or anyplace else, really, except Marc's apartment. Who knew? Maybe this was the universe's way of trying to tell him something.

CHAPTER 14

As usual, we had our big holiday meal on Christmas Eve. Mom made marinated cracked crab and put a standing rib roast with potatoes, carrots, and sprigs of rosemary in the oven. By mid-afternoon, all these tantalizing aromas were floating through the air. Despite our huge breakfast, Cole and I were both pretty fucking ravenous when it came time to sit down to eat.

It did my heart good to see Cole finally unwind, laughing and joking with Mom as if he'd known her for years, although the bottle and a half of cabernet the three of us killed probably had something to do with it. He demolished a helping of crab and two of roast, and looked as if he were contemplating a third before he pushed his plate away. "Better not. I've already made a big enough pig of myself."

Mom laughed. "Don't be silly. I like a man with a good appetite. I'd hate to think I spent all afternoon in the kitchen for nothing."

"This is the best meal I've had since Marc cooked for me on Thanksgiving."

"Did he, now?" She shot me a wink. "Looks like I trained him well."

We kept on chatting until Cole, evidently on auto-pilot despite our conversation this morning, got up and started clearing the table. I was about to protest, but Mom laid a hand on my arm and shook her head. "Let him do it. He obviously needs to feel helpful." Once he started washing up in the kitchen, she added, "He reminds me a lot of Rob."

"Me too." I sighed. "In more ways than one."

"Night terrors?"

"And generalized anxiety, along with occasional flashbacks. He was in Baghdad and Fallujah. From some of the stuff he's told me, I'm actually pretty amazed he hasn't ended up in a rubber room."

She poured them both more wine, emptying out the bottle. "Well, at least you know how to handle it."

"He won't go talk to anybody, though. I've tried to convince him."

"Keep trying. Eventually he'll have to listen."

Oh, if only. Our latest argument on that very subject made me shake my head. "I don't know about that. He's pretty stubborn."

"Just like every other Marine in the whole damn world." She smiled ruefully. "Aren't we a pair? Both drawn to strong, gorgeous men who wear their scars on the inside. But I think this one's a keeper."

I smiled back. "Yeah, I think so too."

Around six o'clock Christmas morning, I woke up with a brilliant idea. I sprang out of bed and pulled on jeans and a sweater, then grabbed Cole's sweats from his bag and sank down on the edge of the bed, gently shaking his shoulder. He rolled onto his back, blinking blearily. "Merry Christmas," he murmured, smiling up at me.

"Merry Christmas." I leaned over to give him a good morning kiss. "C'mon, get dressed. I've got a surprise for you."

"Want to give me a hint?"

"Then it wouldn't be a surprise, would it?"

He sat up with a groan and yanked his sweatshirt over his head. "Just for future reference, I usually prefer my surprises a little later in the day."

I couldn't help feeling a tiny twinge of guilt for waking him so early when it was normally a miracle to get him to sleep past five. But something told me he'd find what I had in mind more than worth it. I left him to finish dressing while I went into the kitchen to get him some coffee.

He chugged it down in one long gulp, shooting me a half-puzzled, half-intrigued glance as I snagged the Jeep's keys off the bedside table. "You're taking me somewhere? At this hour? On Christmas Day?"

"Stow the questions, Marine. And get your shoes on." I waited for him to lace up his Nikes, then pointed at the door. "Move it."

He remained obediently silent as I marched him out to the car, started it up, and headed downtown. It was still dark, but the sky had turned gray at the edges, signaling imminent sunrise. I drove until I reached the public beach, then parked in a lot facing the ocean, with a perfect view of the horizon.

Cole grinned at me as I cut the engine. "Isn't this the wrong direction to watch the sun come up?"

"Well, sort of. The reflection of the sunrise on the water's really pretty. I thought you might like it." I shrugged. "What, too sappy?"

"Don't be stupid. It's romantic. And sweet." He jerked his chin toward the beach. "Let's go sit outside and get a closer look."

I started to shiver the second we climbed out of the car, the freezing, salty-fishy breeze stinging my skin. We ambled a few yards down the beach and plopped onto dry sand. Cole's arm snaked immediately around me. It didn't warm me up that much, but it still felt good.

Heat bloomed on my back as the sun peeked over the mountains behind us, glinting off the water like a sleepy eye just beginning to open. Reminded me of Cole a little while ago. As it rose higher, bathing the world in pale white-gold, then spectacular pinkish-red light, Cole whispered, "I've never really seen a California sunrise before."

"After getting up at the butt-crack of dawn to go running every day?"

"It's not like I was paying attention then. Besides, sitting here watching it with you is a totally different experience."

I leaned my head on his shoulder just as the wind kicked up in earnest, whipping my hair and thrusting an annoying icy finger down the back of my collar. Too late, I yanked up my hood, stifling a grumble. Why did it have to go and ruin a damn near perfect moment?

Then Cole kissed me and said, "Thank you. This was a great gift. And I didn't even have to ask Santa for it."

Well, okay. It was still pretty perfect.

"Why don't you go for a run?" I suggested. "You get antsy when you skip a day, and you've already skipped two."

"Want to come with me?"

Oh, he had to be joking. I shot him a sour look. "You want me to keel over from a heart attack? There's no way I could ever keep up with you. Plus, I'm wearing jeans."

"Okay, I'll take a short one." He stood and started to stretch. "I should be back in about twenty minutes. Go wait in the car. I'd rather not have an icicle for a boyfriend."

He didn't have to tell me twice. I hopped back in the Jeep and switched on the ignition to run the heater for a couple minutes, just long enough to thaw the chill in my bones. I watched Cole jog down the beach until he became this tiny black speck in the distance. Looked like he was about to fall off the edge of the world. Then he turned around and slowly grew larger again, dropping from a jog to a walk, slogging through the sand up to the car with a grin.

"That was a short one?" My gaze swept him from head to toe and back again. He wasn't the least bit sweaty, or even breathing hard.

"Yeah, I usually do five or six miles. This was basically just a warm-up."

"Jesus. I feel like the world's biggest slacker compared to you. I really should get on some kind of fitness program. All this rich holiday food's going to turn me into a butterball."

Cole gazed out the windshield for a long moment. "Well, you know . . . if we were living together, I could take you out running every morning. I'd be happy to help you get started."

There had to be something wrong with my ears. If anyone was going to bring this up, I thought for sure it would've been me. "Are you serious?"

"Why not? We spend most of our evenings together already. Every night I'm at my place, I wish I was at yours. And not just because that fucking band down the hall's giving me a migraine." He looked at me and smiled. "I know we haven't seen seeing each other very long, but all I can think about these days is how much I want to be with you. I don't see that changing anytime soon."

Despite what he'd just said, I half-expected him to burst out laughing and pretend the whole thing had been a joke. But he didn't. In fact, he was giving me this anxious look and rubbing his palms on his sweatpants. Was he afraid I'd turn him down, or secretly hoping I'd let him off the hook?

Problem was, I didn't want to do either. "I feel the same way," I said, then leaned in and kissed him. He let out this little half-amazed, half-joyful sound and wrapped his arms around me, hands sliding up my back to hold me tight. "So, where do you want to live?"

"You'd hate it at my building, believe me. Besides, my apartment's so tiny, we'd be bumping into each other every damn minute."

"Okay, my place it is. But what about your furniture and stuff?"

"It's all thrift store crap. I can donate it back." He beamed.

"I can't believe we're doing this. Hell, I can't even believe I asked you. Or that you actually said yes!"

My heart melted into a puddle at the grin on Cole's face. Drip, drip, drip. "What else can I say? I'm in love with you, you big control-freak-head-case-macho-jerk-Marine." The words popped out before I'd had a chance to weigh them, but when Cole's smile turned positively ecstatic, I knew I'd finally gotten it right.

"I love you too, Marc. I mean, I have to. You're the only guy I've ever met outside the Corps who can keep me in line."

I grinned back. "Well, as long as we agree I outrank you, it's all good."

CHAPTER 15

Cole and Marc decided to head home Saturday morning instead of Sunday, in the hope of missing most of the return holiday traffic. Marc and his mother said their goodbyes while Cole packed up the Jeep. He shut the trunk and turned around to shake her hand and say thank you, only to be knocked for a loop when she threw her arms around him.

"Take care of my boy for me, Cole," she said. "I trust you can do that?"

Blinking hard, he nodded. "Yes, ma'am. I sure will."

"Melinda, please. After all, you're practically my son-in-law." His mouth dropped open as she gave him a wink, then ambled back to her front porch to wave goodbye. He and Marc waved back, climbed into the Jeep, and drove off.

Marc took the wheel for this first leg of their journey out of San Diego and through the LA corridor. They planned to make a pit stop for lunch and gas in Santa Barbara, where Cole would take over—that was, if hunger didn't get the better of them first. They'd been in such a hurry to hit the road, they'd skipped breakfast.

"Okay, that's it," Marc declared after Cole's belly rumbled for the third time before they'd reached the freeway on-ramp. "There's a Starbucks on the next block. Go in and get yourself something. I'm not listening to that for the next two hundred miles."

"And a grande green tea with a blueberry scone for you, right?"

Marc grinned. "Yes, please."

They swung into the parking lot, already packed at barely seven in the morning. Cole piled out of the Jeep and went inside, groaning when he saw the line snaking back to the door. He checked his email on his phone—no word on any of his final grades yet, naturally—then played Tetris until he finally reached the counter.

It took the staff about three minutes to get his house blend, Marc's tea, and a couple of pastries. He paid the barista, then elbowed his way through the crowd to the corner station to stir some raw sugar into his cup and pick up napkins. Then he swung around, eyes sweeping past the dozen or so tables as he sought out the nearest door—

And promptly froze at the sight of a face he'd never expected to see again: the asshole who'd outed him, sitting fifteen feet away, talking on his phone and glancing out the front window. Dressed in civvies, though the tags visible at the open neck of his black polo shirt screamed "active duty." Must've gotten transferred to Pendleton.

Shit. Cole's hands twitched, tightening dangerously around the two cups he held. For a split second, he seriously considered walking up to the guy and flinging the scalding liquid in his face.

Then the guy flicked off his phone, heaved himself from his chair, and walked right toward him. "'Scuse me," he said, flinty gray eyes meeting Cole's for an instant before he reached past him to toss his cup in the trash. With that, he turned and headed for the men's room.

Cole followed him halfway to the restroom door before his rational mind kicked in. What was he going to do, get in a damn fistfight in front of a store full of witnesses? Get his ass hauled off to jail and make Marc come bail him out?

Every instinct told him to go, yet he remained frozen to the spot until the guy emerged, forehead crinkling as his now-puzzled gaze lighted on Cole again. Cole could practically see the hamster wheel in his tiny brain start to spin. Best get out of here before the guy figured it out or Cole did something stupid. He swung around and bolted for the door.

"Okay, what's wrong?" I turned down the music so I wouldn't get drowned out by "Born in the USA." "You haven't said a word in the last fifty miles."

Cole rubbed at his eyes, his jaw tightening. "I'd rather not discuss it."

"Nope, sorry. I'm not sitting next to Stonewall Jackson for the next eight hours. Everything was fine until you went into Starbucks, then you come stomping out all silent and pissed off. Talk to me, Cole. What gives?"

Dead quiet. Evidently it was going to take an atomic blast to get it out of him. Or maybe just a smile and a ridiculously empty threat. "Do you want me to pull over and make you walk home? Because I will."

One corner of Cole's mouth fought a futile battle not to quirk upward. "That's my car you're driving, remember?"

"Possession of the wheel is nine-tenths of the law." I switched off the CD player. "No more Bruce until you tell me. C'mon, it can't be that bad."

"Not bad so much as . . . fucking weird. And confusing." He pulled his cup out of the holder but didn't drink, just stared down at it as if it held the secrets of the universe, ground and brewed from fair trade beans. "The guy who outed me was in there."

"*What?*" I threw him a quick glance. "Are you sure it was him?"

"Oh, yeah. Believe me, I'll never forget that face. But apparently the same doesn't go for him. He got as close to me as you are right now, and . . . nothing. The guy ruined my whole fucking life, and he didn't even remember me."

The pain and frustration in his trembling voice tore at my heart. "I hope you didn't do anything foolish."

"I didn't do anything, period. I was too damn stunned. For a year and a half I've been rehearsing what I'd say if I ever saw him again. But when the moment of truth came, I just stood there like an idiot."

"Well, I think you handled it the best way possible. He's caused you more than enough grief already."

Cole gazed out the window for a few silent minutes, watching other cars speed past us. "You know, I think I get it now. I've been looking at my life all wrong. Glass half empty, when it should be half full. I've got everything going for me, but I was too bullheaded to see it. That guy didn't ruin my life. It was my choice to tell my CO the truth about me, and I'm glad I did. If I hadn't, I wouldn't have ended up in Berkeley. I wouldn't have met you. And I wouldn't have just had the best fucking Christmas since I was ten."

Did he really just say he was *glad* to have exchanged the Corps for me? Relief and stunned gratitude swept over me so strongly they left me dizzy. Breathing deep, I tightened my hands on the wheel until it passed. Then, with a smile, I switched the music back on. "Maybe you should send that guy flowers."

"I would, if I could remember his name."

We both burst out laughing, and sailed up the freeway toward home.

Chapter 15

When the alarm went off at five, I lifted one drowsy eyelid with a groan.

"Aw, c'mon, don't give me that," Cole said, swinging his legs over the side of the bed. "Up and at 'em."

"Won't fucking burn the same amount of calories?"

"Unh-uh. I'm not letting you distract me with sex again." He laughed and gave my butt a playful slap. "What's the problem? I thought you wanted to get in shape."

"I forgot about the hauling-ass-out-of-bed-at-an-ungodly-hour part."

"If we wait 'til tonight, you'll be tired from work and bitching at me about losing writing time. So quit complaining and get dressed." He sprang to his feet and pulled on his sweats, undeterred by the impressive erection bulging at the front of his pants. One look, and I practically drooled. Ah, the joys of having a boyfriend who woke up hard. Not that he'd give me a chance to enjoy it this morning.

I threw on a raggedy old pair of gray sweatpants, my navy blue Cal hoodie, and the same black sneakers I wore to work every day. The frosty January air smacked me in the face with a cruel backhand, though the chill faded pretty quickly as Cole led me through his usual stretching exercises. Then we started off at a slow jog down the street, gradually picking up speed.

We alternated jogging and walking for a close to a mile, but I still ended up drenched in sweat, every muscle in my body screaming. Gasping for breath, I crumpled onto a deserted bus stop bench. "Sorry," I panted, "but I'm gonna have to rest."

Cole immediately halted and swung around. "God, your face is all red. I knew I shouldn't have pushed you so hard your first time out."

Pushed me so hard? He wasn't even out of breath. As if I didn't feel like enough of a lazy ass already. "I'll be okay, just give me a couple minutes."

He dropped to his knees beside me, pressing two fingers to the throbbing pulse in my throat. "Better not. Your heart's already racing. Let's go over to that coffee house and get you something to drink. I don't want you to dehydrate."

"What about your workout?"

"Don't worry about me. C'mon." Linking arms, we crossed the street—or rather, he crossed the street, dragging my wrung out carcass behind him—and headed for the coffee house. Cole deposited me at a table, then stood in line to get me a cup of tea. It was so hot I had to remove the lid and wait for it to stop steaming before taking my first sip.

"Thanks," I rasped. My throat felt as if it'd been scrubbed out with sandpaper, but at least there wasn't a whole set of encyclopedias crushing my chest anymore. "Talk about embarrassing. I didn't think I was this badly out of shape."

"It's my fault. I should've started you off more slowly." Cole fiddled with a plastic coffee-stirrer, his brows knit in thought. "Why don't we join that gym a couple blocks over? They've got treadmills and stationary bikes and all kinds of weight machines. We can design a program that'll get you working at your own pace."

"Isn't it expensive?"

"They might have some specials going. I'll check it out on my way home from class today." He grinned. "Home. *Our* home. I'm still getting used to saying it. But . . ."

"But what?"

"Well, maybe we should think about getting a bigger place. At least a one bedroom. Studying at the table'll do me for now, but I wouldn't mind having my own desk. And what about a decent-sized kitchen, so we don't have to eat out so much?"

My cup froze halfway to my lips. The last few days since he'd moved in had washed over me like some hazy, euphoric dream. Any minute I expected to wake up and find myself alone, with only the comforter and Thomas to keep me warm. Did this really mean he wanted to make our current living arrangements permanent?

He looked so damn happy, my heart couldn't help but start skipping again. Luckily, this time I didn't feel like I was ready to pass out. "That's a great idea, but . . ."

His smile crumpled. Now it was his turn to say, "But what?"

"Are you sure you're ready?"

"Are *you?*" he shot back, both hands tightening around his coffee cup.

Honestly, I had no fucking clue how to answer, but I'd let the silence drag on too long. "Why don't we talk about it again closer to the end of the term? We've both got too much going on right now."

"Sure." A half-stifled sigh. "Whatever you want."

Shit. Too late for a do-over now. I knocked back my last sip of tea, and we got up to leave. All I wanted was a long, hot shower, though it hardly seemed like I'd earned it. Between making Cole stay behind to babysit me and putting the kibosh on looking for a new place, I obviously needed "World's Shittiest Boyfriend" tattooed across my forehead. "Why don't you finish your run?" I suggested.

"S'okay, I don't have to. Skipping a day won't kill me."

"Go *on*. I think I can manage to walk home by myself." I forced a smile in the face of his hesitant concern, then figured, *Fuck it*, clutched his sweatshirt with both hands, and hauled him in for a kiss.

When his arms snaked around me, I practically slumped

against him in relief. "It's okay, I get it," he murmured. "I'll leave you alone for a while."

"Look, I don't mean to—"

"Yeah, you do. I know you pretty well by now. You need your space. You haven't lived with anybody in a while, and I never have. Guess it's gonna take us some time to adjust."

So he really did get it—or at least he seemed to. Thank God he wasn't mad. "Well, hurry back," I said, flashing him a smile. "Who knows? I might have a surprise for you."

The twinkle in those blue, blue eyes of his told me he knew exactly what I was thinking. "I can hardly wait." Another kiss, and then he turned and started jogging down the street in the opposite direction.

I waited until he faded off into the distance before heading home. I worked up another good sweat just from walking, but my shower got delayed by Thomas greeting me at the door, demanding morning pets and kibble. I gave him plenty of both, then staggered to the bathroom for my own reward. The hot spray flowed down my body like liquid bliss, dissolving every bone and muscle into jelly. I slouched against the cool tiles, too drained to move.

That is, until the shower door opened and in stepped Cole, naked and smiling. The scent of his sweat tickled my nostrils and perked me up *all* over. "So this is my surprise, huh?" he growled, reaching for my cock.

I let him jerk me to the brink of orgasm before knocking his hands away. I wasn't ready for it to be over so quickly—and besides, I wanted to give him some of his own back first. Time to disabuse him of the notion that he was in control here. Shoving him against the wall, I let my hands roam over his slippery torso as I sank to my knees to suck the fat, rosy crown of his cock into my mouth.

I gripped his thighs and took my time blowing him, the warm water raining over us both. I worked him to the edge, then eased off until he gazed down at me, a hungry, desperate plea shining in his eyes. With an impatient grunt, he seized my wrist and yanked me up and out of the shower, dragged me down the hall past a scattered trail of his discarded sweats, socks and sneakers, and tossed me on the bed.

So much for regaining control—not that I gave a fuck at this point. I'd barely rolled onto my stomach before Cole's face burrowed between my cheeks, his breath hot and heavenly on my sensitized skin as he licked and opened me. Lube-slicked fingers pushed inside, followed by his hard, ready cock, and soon he was happily pounding me into the mattress.

Our first week living together. *Jesus*. If it got much better, I didn't think I could stand it.

CHAPTER 17

They fell into the habit of having supper at the diner a couple nights a week. Cole liked the food and shooting the breeze with Terry. It was nice having something special to look forward to after a long day in class. Seeing Marc's face when he walked through the front door never failed to make him grin like an idiot. And sitting across the table from him . . . well, nothing had ever felt more natural and comfortable to Cole in his entire life.

"So when's your birthday?" he asked.

Marc glanced up from his Cobb salad, wiping his mouth on his napkin. "October twelfth. Why?"

"Oh." Damn. He'd hoped it'd be during the summer so they could take a short trip somewhere. "Guess that gives me plenty of time to think of what to get you."

"Cole, you don't have to buy me gifts. I've already got everything I need."

"But I thought you liked it when I brought you flowers and stuff."

"I love it when you do romantic, unexpected things. But I don't want you to feel like you have to make a big deal out of birthdays or holidays. It should be a joy, not an obligation. Not something you do because you think you have to prove you love me. Which you don't." He took another bite, chewing slowly. "Prove, I mean; not love," he added with a smile. "However, if you insist on doing something for me, I know what I'd ask for."

And so did Cole. Marc had been hinting around at it for

months now, ever since the night he'd freaked out in that alley. "I don't need to see a fucking doctor. I've only had nightmares a couple of times since we moved in together."

"But you still flip your shit every time a car backfires, and we can't even go to a movie because the crowds make you nervous."

"It'll get better on its own. It has to, eventually."

"Maybe, maybe not. Even if it does, it could end up taking years. Do you really want to wait that long?" Marc reached across the table to clasp Cole's hand. "Let me make you an appointment at campus health services, okay? If you want me to go with you, I will. At least get them to refill your Xanax. You ran out weeks ago."

Oh, great. Now Marc had made it impossible for him to refuse without sounding like the most obstinate asshole of all time. Which didn't mean he wasn't going to try. "I don't have time to cool my heels in some waiting room. My schedule's crazy enough as it is."

"You've got time to drop by here to say hi to me on your way home every day, but you can't spare an hour for a doctor's appointment?"

"Marc, c'mon—"

"Stop it, okay? You're a grown man, Cole. You know you've got a problem. You could've had it seen to months ago, but you didn't. What're you so afraid of?"

Cole grasped his fork until the metal bit into his palm. Jesus, why couldn't Marc just leave him be? Stupid of him to have hoped everything would be a walk in the park once they'd moved in together.

Truthfully, though, Marc's persistence was kind of a relief. Just like following orders. No matter how tough the job, when he knew he had no choice, he simply buckled down and did it. And that's what he was facing here. Obviously, Marc was going to keep hammering at him until he got his way.

"Okay," Cole replied at last. "One appointment. That's all I'm agreeing to."

"That's all I'm asking. Thank you." Marc's fingers tightened around his. God, he reminded Cole of his own mother. They shared the same steely backbone, coupled with a full, generous heart. How the hell had he gotten so lucky? "I'll call first thing in the morning and set it up."

The clinic had a cancellation for the following Monday afternoon, so I took it. Cole's eyebrows shot up when I told him, but then he nodded and said, "Okay. Might as well get it over with." Not exactly reassuring, but at least he wasn't trying to renege.

He turned down my offer to go with him, which didn't really surprise me. Still, I'd hoped he'd call me at work to let me know how it had gone. When he didn't, I called him. It went straight to voicemail, which didn't necessarily mean anything; he always turned off his ringer before he went into class, and most of the time he forgot to turn it back on again. I left a short message.

But he didn't call me back. My stomach twisted up in knots as I sprinted home, only a tiny bit relieved when I saw the kitchen light shining through the curtains. I charged through the front door to find Cole studying at the table while Thomas snoozed at his feet. Just like any other evening.

It wasn't until I came over to give him a kiss that I noticed two slips of white paper lying near his open textbook, with the clinic's name, address and phone number printed at the top. A prescription for Xanax, and some other drug I'd never heard of before.

"It's an antidepressant," Cole supplied. "I don't know why

they want me to take it. I told them I've never been happier in my life."

Flattering, though not terribly soothing, given the circumstances. I pulled out the other chair and sat down. "Well, it couldn't hurt to try it, right?"

"But I don't *need* it!" He slammed his book closed with a thump that made poor Thomas hop to his feet and skitter away.

"It might help your concentration," I said gently. "And it'll definitely help you sleep better."

"I sleep fine."

"Bullshit. You think I don't hear you rattling around in the kitchen at all hours? Even when you don't have nightmares, you still hardly ever sleep through the night."

"Only because Thomas keeps waking me up to feed him."

"Nice try, but he was snuggled under the covers with me the last time I heard you." Deep breath, and then, "There's nothing shameful or weak in acknowledging you need help. You didn't have a problem taking the Xanax before. Why is this new drug any different?"

"Because I only took Xanax when I needed it. The other one I have to take every day. I don't want to use it as a crutch."

"It's not a crutch. It's just something to help you cope." I took a look at the prescriptions again, though the doctor's loopy scrawl made them a bit hard to decipher. "They usually start you off at the lowest dose. Maybe you won't need any more than that."

"Sounds like you've got experience with this kind of stuff."

"Yeah, I do," I admitted. "My first year at Berkeley was pretty rough. I'd never been away from home before. I missed my mom. I almost flunked a couple of classes. If it weren't for Zoloft, I might've taken a dive off the administration building. Which is why they've got those bars up at the top, by the way.

They used to have a whole slew of suicide attempts around finals every semester."

Cole rubbed a hand over his face. "Jesus, Marc, I'm not suicidal."

"But you're still suffering. There's no reason you need to white-knuckle your way through this. If the pills can help you deal with the stress, then take the fucking pills." I scooped up the two prescriptions and tucked them in my backpack. "I'll drop these off at the drugstore tomorrow, okay?"

"Okay." He drummed his fingers on the table for a second, then reached into his back pocket and pulled out another slip of paper. "They gave me a referral to a private therapist. He's an ex-Army shrink who specializes in treating PTSD."

"If that's your way of asking if you should go see him, you already know my answer."

"I just don't know if I can talk about this shit with some stranger."

A fair point, since I could barely even get him to talk to me about it. "Will you give it a try? For me, if not for yourself?"

"In other words, shut up and listen to you, huh?" he retorted, cracking a tiny smile.

With a mock roll of my eyes, I came over to sit on his lap and wrap my arms around him. "You're my big, strong man, and I love you. But you don't have to be so fucking macho and in control all the time. Let me take care of you." Not that he actually would, but I needed to say it. "That's what I'm here for."

Cole was still snoring away beside me when I opened my eyes around seven. Only a couple weeks since he'd started taking his new meds, but now he slept like a boulder—a full eight hours every night, with no bad dreams. I'd never heard of anti-depressants working so fast, but it was plain he'd been horribly serotonin-deprived. I smiled and kissed him gently on the shoulder, then threw on my robe, grabbed my laptop, and took it into the kitchen to work.

I'd kept going with the journaling project I'd started a few weeks ago, keeping a daily account of Cole's and my life together. Still wasn't sure what I'd do with it, if anything. I liked having a piece of writing that was completely mine—a private space where I could ramble on without worrying about weaving a story or having to make sense. Maybe I'd show it to Cole someday. But right now it served as a way for me clear my mind before moving on to my latest manuscript.

After an hour or so I got up to brew myself some tea. As the kettle started to whistle, a telltale groan wafted in from the next room. I took the kettle off the burner before poking my head around the corner. "Sorry," I said. "Didn't mean to wake you."

Cole yawned and shot a glance at the clock. "You should've woken me an hour ago. I wanted to go running."

"Easy, tiger. It's Sunday, remember? A day of rest and relaxation, even if you think they're both dirty words."

"Then what're you doing up already?" God, he was using that slow, sexy tone that brought out his Carolina drawl. It always sounded stronger in the morning, with his voice still husky from sleep.

"Just getting in a little writing time. No big deal."

"You and your writing." He snorted. "Now I know how my mama feels every time football season rolls around."

"I'm all done for now," I replied with a smile.

"Fine, then. Get your cute little ass over here *pronto*."

I couldn't drop my robe and crawl back in bed fast enough. His arm slid around my waist as he rolled on top of me, his hard-on poking my belly. I'd been afraid the antidepressants would kill his sex drive, but thankfully, this new breed of SSRI had the opposite effect. He took it at bedtime, and it usually knocked him out within half an hour. Didn't keep him from waking up raring to go in the morning, though, which suited me just fine.

His hot wet kisses made my head swim, but when he started working his way lower, I gave him a gentle push until he landed on his back and let me climb on top. No resistance, just a question in his gaze and a soft smile turning up the corners of his mouth. I snagged the bottle of baby oil and squirted some onto his chest. His head lolled back, eyelids drooping as I massaged it into his skin.

I'd never seen him so relaxed before, the tight, tense lines around his eyes and mouth completely erased. He laid there and let me do what I wanted, my palms gliding over firm muscles from belly to shoulder and back again. I had a feeling he wouldn't mind if I sucked him off, but today I was in the mood for something different—which didn't rule out a little teasing before the main event.

I decided to lavish some attention on his balls, painting them with wide, leisurely swipes of my tongue as I inhaled deeply, drinking in his scent. My hands were still slippery with oil, so I straightened up a moment to wipe them off and grab the lube, then skimmed my index finger up the crack of his ass and swirled it around his hole. Despite being sorely tempted, I didn't dare push inside, not if I wanted him to last much longer. I had plans for that big, beautiful dick of his.

Plans that included making him watch while I rolled off and fingered my own ass, getting myself ready for him to fuck me. And there came that tension again, written in the taut line of his jaw and fistfuls of bed covers clutched in both hands. Time to help him de-stress the best way I knew.

Condom on, lube quickly applied, I straddled his hips again, lowering myself onto his cock. The burn of initial entry swiftly gave way to a sweet ache that seemed to go on forever as I rocked back and forth, taking my time. Cole moaned and grasped my waist, though I batted his other hand away when he reached for my cock.

"Relax," I half-murmured, half-growled. "You're not running this fuck, I am. So lie back and enjoy it."

With the world's deepest groan, he settled into the mattress and let me take over. It was actually rather touching. I'd only caught glimpses of his submissive side before, like the other night in the shower, or back when I'd first fingered him. He still hadn't let me fuck him yet, and while I could hardly wait, I had no plans to press the issue. He'd ask for it when he was ready. Just like I was ready for him to come inside me right *now*.

I sped up, rocking him hard until he gave me what I wanted. My own orgasm caught me off-guard, bursting forth the moment my fingers touched my cock, so intense it left my ears ringing.

"That's one hell of a wake-up call," Cole mumbled as I crumpled at his side. About ten seconds later, I heard him start to snore again. Didn't take me long to follow suit.

CHAPTER 18

Cole had only visited a psychiatrist's office once before, back at Camp Lejeune, and not by his own choice. He'd been ordered to report there for evaluation while his separation was pending, and the way that'd turned out didn't make him eager to repeat the experience. But this was for treatment, not evaluation. Besides, he'd promised Marc he'd give it his best shot.

So he took a seat in the tiny waiting room with "Ethan West, M.D., Ph.D." on the front door. No receptionist—not that he'd expected one, since Dr. West had answered the phone himself when Cole had called to make his appointment. Instinctively, he scoped out the exits—two doors, one leading to the hallway, the other presumably to the inner office; and an unlatched window overlooking the parking lot. His gaze skated over the pretty but unmemorable watercolors hanging on the far wall, and finally landed on three framed diplomas. Bachelor's and doctorate in psychology from Northwestern, medical degree from Johns Hopkins. Well, at least the guy had impressive credentials.

He scooped up a dog-eared copy of *TIME* and thumbed through it, but nothing held his interest for more than a few seconds. The clock over the office door ticked like a fucking bomb counting down. Pulse suddenly racing, he tossed the magazine aside and sprang to his feet, rubbing his clammy palms on his jeans as he paced. Why the hell hadn't he let Marc come with him? He'd have given anything for someone to talk to right now.

As if on cue, the office door opened, and a tall, fiftyish guy appeared. Wavy salt-and-pepper hair. Clean, pressed jeans and a pale blue dress shirt with the sleeves rolled up. Big toothy smile. "Cole Hammond?"

"Yeah." He wasn't sure whether to offer to shake hands or not, but Dr. West extending his own hand quickly settled that dilemma. He had a firm, reassuring grip, though it didn't do much to ease the trembling in Cole's fingers.

"I'm Ethan West. C'mon in and make yourself comfortable." The doctor ushered him into the office and shut the door. Slightly nicer furniture in here, including a comfy-looking leather sofa and chairs. An oak desk stood in the corner beside a sliding glass door that opened onto a rock garden. Cole had to smile at the three walls' worth of crammed bookshelves. Reminded him of Marc's—no, *his* and Marc's living room.

Framed snapshots perched on the desk and atop the shelves. A glimpse of Army fatigues caught Cole's eye, drawing him in for a closer look. It was a photo of Dr. West, his dark hair marking it as an old picture, along with two other guys. They sat in a Jeep against an arid desert backdrop, arms around each other's shoulders. Just looking at it made Cole's throat go tight. He remembered what that sense of camaraderie and brotherhood felt like. The bone-deep knowledge that his unit was right there with him, ready to back him up, defend him to the death. The thought of never having that again made every fiber of him ache.

"Desert Storm?" he asked finally.

The doctor nodded, taking a seat directly across from the couch. "I was stationed at Walter Reed for the last few years of my stint, but I did get to make a few excursions into the field. Wish I could've spent more time there."

Cole couldn't help snorting. "Don't sound so disappointed. Believe me, you didn't miss much."

"Aside from . . ." He scooped up a yellow scratch pad with some notes scribbled on it. "Nightmares, periods of intense anxiety, and flashbacks?"

Everything Cole had told him over the phone, when it had all seemed so easy. When he didn't have to look the guy in the face. A hard knot congealing in his belly, he ambled to the couch and sank down heavily. "Nothing like getting right to it, huh?"

The doctor smiled again, all sincere and disarming. Did they teach a class in that at shrink school? "Hey, it's your hour. We can talk about anything you want." He set down the scratch pad and leaned back in his chair. "But why don't we start with what motivated you to seek out therapy?"

"What, you mean bad dreams and panic attacks aren't enough?"

"Those are symptoms, not reasons. Didn't you say something about your partner prompting you to call?"

Cole hesitated, then gave a grudging nod. Bad enough he had to be here at all. Twice as bad acknowledging that he had to be strong-armed into it. Still, if this was going to work, he should probably be honest. "It was Marc's idea, yeah."

"So you're only here because he gave you an ultimatum?"

"Marc doesn't do ultimatums. He just insists a lot." A chuckle rumbled up from his chest, catching him by surprise.

"Well, if you're only doing this to placate him, it won't be of much benefit. Therapy's a long process requiring patience and commitment. If you're not ready for it, don't force yourself, even for his sake."

There it was—the perfect out. All he had to do was get up and leave. He wanted to—God, how he wanted to!—but his legs refused to move. What was he going to do, go home and tell Marc he'd broken his promise and bailed without even giving it one full session? Or pretend he was still coming and kill an extra hour hanging out in the library every week instead? No, he couldn't do that. He couldn't lie to Marc, and he couldn't disappoint him either.

He stared at the floor. "So, doc—"

"Ethan, please."

That brought Cole up short. He'd never called a doctor by his first name before. He'd never called the USMC doctors anything but 'sir.' "You sure?"

"If you're more comfortable calling me 'doctor,' go ahead. But I prefer to keep things informal. After twenty-five years in the service, I've had my fill of standing on ceremony."

"Fair enough. So, how does all this work?"

"Any way you want it to. Like I said, it's your hour. But since I don't have access to your service record, you'll have to give me some background." Ethan reached for the pad again. "Start wherever you like, but be warned—I love asking questions."

Cole huffed out another chuckle, though this one sounded more like a strangled bark. "You've got no idea what you're in for."

Smile fading, Ethan skewered him with a steady, dead-serious gaze. "I've spent the better part of the last two decades listening to soldiers tell me about their battlefield experiences. There's not much that can shock me."

"We'll see. I'm a Marine, remember?"

One salt-and-pepper eyebrow quirked up. "And you jarheads all think you're so tough."

"That's because we are, compared to you Army pussies."

They both laughed. Cole slumped back against the couch cushions and rubbed a hand through his hair, the tension inside him finally starting to dissolve. Maybe this wouldn't be such a fucking ordeal after all.

Cole could hear Marc typing away on his laptop the second he got the apartment door open. He dropped his jacket and backpack on the kitchen table and continued on into the living room, coming up behind Marc to slide his hands onto his shoulders. "Writing again, I see. Or should that be, *still?*"

Marc grinned and swung around in his seat. "Always, more like. So how'd your first appointment go?"

"It went." He dropped onto the edge of the couch. "I mean, he's a nice enough guy. Seems easy to talk to. We'll see where it goes, I guess."

"Sounds like you're describing a bad date."

"An expensive date, and I didn't even get laid. Speaking of . . ." He grabbed Marc's hand and tried to tug him to the couch, but Marc wouldn't budge. In fact, he actually pulled away.

"Look," Marc said, flashing him a contrite smile. "I really need to get these revisions done. They were due last week. But I'll make it up to you soon as I'm finished, okay?"

Cole didn't smile back. "And then next week you'll start something new. Jesus, don't you ever take more than a few days off?"

That *look* crept onto Marc's face: that strained, long-suffering grimace he wore whenever they argued. "C'mon, Cole, this is my job. My *real* job. I don't want to still be waiting tables for a living when I'm forty fucking years old."

"I know you think I don't get it, but I do. You want to be a professional writer. That's great. But why does it have to take up so much of your time? It wasn't so bad when I first moved in, but now every day when I get home, you're writing. We have dinner, then you go right back to it. Can't you do it in the morning instead?"

"What, in between tagging along with you to the gym before I head off to the diner?" With a sharp huff, Marc shut his laptop and pushed back in his chair, arms crossed over his chest. "I'm not a morning person, Cole. You know that."

Oh, that was bullshit. He'd woken up plenty of times and found Marc writing. But pointing that out would just prolong the argument. "Fine," he said, heaving himself off the bed. "Keep on working. I'm gonna go study."

He had his nose buried in his tort law textbook when a familiar shadow fell across the table, and Marc's knuckles brushed his cheek. "Sorry," he murmured. "I get a little obsessed with my work sometimes."

"A *little?*" Cole echoed, catching hold of Marc's hand. "Not to sound jealous of your books, but I'm starting to wonder if you care more about them than me."

"Of course not! But Cole, you have to understand, I'm used to keeping my own schedule, doing what I want when I want. I'm a night owl, and you're used to getting up at the stroke of five. It's a big change. You need to cut me some slack, okay?"

"Goes both ways, doesn't it?"

"Like I just said, I'm sorry." He leaned down for a kiss, slow and sweet, an apology better than words could convey. "I *promise* I'll take a break as soon as I finish with this book. Two more days, and it'll be on my editor's desk and out of my hair. And when I get my first royalty check for it, we'll go over to the city for dinner. Anyplace you want, my treat." He grinned. "Deal?"

Oh, no fucking fair. How was he supposed to refuse in the face of that adorable, happy smile? "Deal." This time he kissed Marc, giving him a swat on the ass for good measure. "Now get back in there and finish the damn thing so we can have some quality time."

"Yes *sir*."

Marc disappeared into the living room and started tapping away on the laptop again. Cole tried to go back to studying, but it was no use. He read the same paragraph three times and still had no fucking idea what it said. The instant he pushed his book aside, Thomas hopped into his lap, demanding attention. Cole stroked his soft fur absently, mulling over the day as that knot in his gut clenched again. Just when he thought things were getting better, in rolled another punch. He was getting pretty fucking tired of dodging them.

CHAPTER 19

Terry exhaled a long tendril of cigarette smoke and cast a stink-eyed glance in my direction as I breezed into the kitchen to pick up an order. "You know, I think there's a law against whistling this early in the day."

Oh, she had to be joking. "I was whistling?"

"Either that, or you've sprung a leak somewhere." She stamped out her Marlboro with a lopsided grin. "Don't get me wrong—I'm happy you're happy, hon. But your Cole Porter's not doing much for my headache."

"Sorry about that." I scooped up my armload of plates and headed out front to deliver them, ambling up to the counter once I was done. Terry had gone to the register to ring up a customer. It was slow this morning, despite the bright May sunshine streaming down outside. Maybe I'd take a walk during my break. Now that I'd been working out with Cole at the gym for the past few months, I actually looked forward to physical activity, even the outside-the-bedroom variety.

"So how's your sweetie doing?" Terry prompted, pouring herself a cup of decaf. "Still seeing that therapist?"

I hesitated a moment before nodding. I didn't want to get into this with Terry, grateful as I was for her concern. "Believe it or not, yeah. He hasn't even complained about going lately."

"Well, that's encouraging. He sure laughs a lot more now than he used to. Does he tell you what he talks about?"

"No, not really."

"Aren't you curious?"

Sure I was, especially after sessions when he stomped home with every muscle in his body rigid and a grim, taut-lipped

"Don't talk to me" expression on his face. He'd throw on his sweats and go out for a long run, then come back calmer, more focused, even strangely at peace. No way was I about to mess with that. "It's his shit to work through, Ter. If he wants to tell me, he will."

"Wish I had it in me to be so sickeningly mature. Which probably explains my two divorces." She patted my shoulder, then went to seat a pair of new customers who'd just walked through the door.

The breakfast shift dragged on into the lunch shift, which dragged into the early dinner shift. Business actually started to pick up a bit. I hadn't expected to see Cole here tonight, so when he showed up around five with that familiar stormy look on his face, I made a beeline for him and asked, "What's the matter?"

"Didn't you see today's paper?" He fumbled in the messy stack of newsprint on the counter, yanking out the front page. And there it was, right below the masthead in screaming bold type: "House Set to Vote on DADT Repeal."

All I could do was stare, the newspaper clutched in my curling fingers. "Guess there's a downside to not owning a TV."

"Or being so busy studying. I haven't looked at the online news for a fucking week." Cole glanced at the headline, shaking his head. "I can't believe this."

"You think it'll really happen?"

"Who the hell knows? They've been making noise about it ever since Obama got elected."

Terry arched an eyebrow at me as more customers filed in. The place was filling up fast. "I should get back to work. We'll talk about it when I get home, all right?"

"I have to hit the library first, but I'll try not to be late. See you at home." And out the door he strode, without bothering to kiss me goodbye. Even considering how preoccupied he was, it still fucking hurt.

To my surprise and relief, he came back a few minutes before seven, wearing a distinctly contrite expression. He and Terry chatted while I went to clock out, and then we started off home together. His fingers found mine as we strolled down the street, clasping them tightly. "Sorry I was such an asshole earlier."

"S'okay. That had to be pretty big shock."

"It's all anybody talked about at school today. I was totally fucking blindsided. I didn't think it would happen while I still had time . . ."

I shot him a puzzled look. "While you still had time for what?"

"Nothing."

Neither of us spoke another word the rest of the way home. Cole sat down at the table to study while I fixed us a quick beef-and-veggie stir-fry for dinner. He set aside his books as I brought our plates over and sat down. I waited for him to say something, but he just picked up his fork and started eating.

All right, then. Guess it was up to me. "Tell me the truth, Cole. If they repeal it, are you thinking about rejoining?"

He finished chewing, then took a sip of water. "Look, even if the House passes it, it's still got to get through the Senate. They're so backed up, it could take months. Hell, it's taken them sixteen fucking years to get this far. I'm not holding my breath yet."

"That's not what I asked." Again, I waited for him to reply. This time, his silence and his averted gaze told me all I needed to know. Suddenly I felt very grateful to be sitting down.

"I don't get it," I whispered finally. "You gave them twelve years of your life, and they treated you like a damn criminal. Why would you want to go back to that?"

He still couldn't bring himself to look at me. "I didn't say I wanted to go back."

"You didn't have to." I took a bite of my stir-fry, but my stomach was roiling so much I almost heaved it back up. I wobbled to my feet and dumped the food in the trash, then set my plate in the sink and went into the living room. But I just sat there staring at my laptop screen until Cole came up behind me. He didn't try to touch me. I wasn't sure whether to feel grateful for that, or utterly fucking abandoned.

"Marc, c'mon. I told you before we got together that being a Marine's the only career I ever wanted. A few pills and shrink visits aren't gonna change that."

I couldn't look at him. This hurt bad enough without actually seeing his face. "You said you weren't going anywhere. You *promised*."

"And I haven't! I'm right here, if you'll just look me in the eye and *talk* to me!"

Somehow, I did, breathing deep to stay calm when all I really wanted was to fling myself at him and pound my fists on his chest. "You've been making progress with your recovery. You've finally hit your stride at school. Do you really want to wash it all down the drain so they can ship you back to Iraq to get your ass shot off?"

"Who says they'll send me to Iraq? They're supposed to start pulling the combat troops out of there soon anyway. There's plenty of other places I could be posted."

"What, like Afghanistan? You're infantry, Cole. They go where the fighting is. Five tours, and you made it home without a scratch. Think you'll be so lucky this time?"

"Christ, stop blowing everything out of proportion! They haven't even voted on the fucking bill yet!" He stomped into the kitchen and started washing up, plates and silverware clattering angrily while I sat staring at my screen some more, clutching at my laptop so hard the casing creaked.

At last I got up and drifted to the doorway, arms folded over my chest. "Does this mean we're over?"

His startled blue gaze locked on mine. "Why would you think that?"

"Well, I doubt they'll let you pack me away in your knapsack. Or move me into base housing as your spouse."

He wiped his hands on a towel and came over to me. My heart almost bashed a hole through my chest when he pulled me close. Despite myself, I looped my arms around his neck and held him as if it were the last time.

"When I say I love you, I mean it," Cole murmured. "As far as I'm concerned, we're together for life."

"So I guess you'll tell the Corps to mail me your coffin?"

"Will you stop worrying? Nothing's changed yet, and if the powers that be in Washington have their way, nothing will change." He kissed me softly, cracking a tiny smile. "I don't plan on leaving, now or anytime in the future."

So he said, but even his apparent sincerity wasn't enough to scrub the rest of the evening from my mind. Once bedtime came, I burrowed under the covers and turned to face the wall, shrugging Cole off when he tried to spoon behind me. I lay there for a long time after he'd drifted off, my thoughts racing. I had to go take one of his Xanax before I calmed down enough to sleep.

The House passed the bill—and then, as Cole had predicted, nothing else happened. It got sent to the Senate and languished there, and no doubt would indefinitely. Cole's heart died a little when he read the news, but he didn't have time to brood about it. He had papers to write, exams to take.

He ambled home with an actual spring in his step on his

last day of classes, doing a double-take at the all-too-familiar tap-tapping of Marc working away at his laptop. He dropped his backpack on the kitchen table before venturing in to see what was what. "Aren't you supposed to be at the diner?"

Marc glanced up, but kept on typing. "I switched days off with Terry. Need to get this new novella finished."

"I don't remember you mentioning it."

"Sorry, thought I did. I've only got a few more pages, so if you don't mind . . ."

Didn't need to club him over the head twice. He shoved his hands in his pockets and beat a hasty retreat back to the kitchen. With no studying to do, he felt distinctly at loose ends. Maybe he'd go for a run. It was a nice day out, sunny and warm with crystal-clear blue skies. Might as well enjoy it.

He pushed well past his usual route, running until his lungs and muscles screamed for mercy. Soaked through, he ended up walking most of the way back. He found Marc at the kitchen table, nibbling on a salad he'd brought home from the diner the other night.

"Did you finish?" Cole asked, coming over to give him a kiss. Was he imagining it, or did Marc just flinch? Sure, he reeked of sweat, but that had never bothered Marc before. In fact, most of the time it turned him on.

"Yup, all done except for editing. There's more salad in the fridge if you want it."

"I'm gonna grab a shower first."

He rinsed off quickly and threw on fresh clothes, then padded barefoot to the kitchen to fix himself a plate. He'd never been particularly fond of salads, but Marc was starting to convert him. Couldn't keep devouring red meat and fatty fried foods and expect to stay healthy.

Once he sat down, he noticed Marc was skimming the newspaper. "When did we start getting the *Chronicle*?"

"We didn't. It's yesterday's paper. I swiped it from the diner."

"You can read the news online, you know."

Marc shot him a sharp look. "What's wrong with reading the paper?"

"You're just not in the habit, is all. Unless you picked it up to look at the local classifieds." When Marc's forehead went all crinkly, he added, "For apartment listings."

"Oh. Yeah." Marc folded the front page in half and laid it on the table. "Maybe we should wait."

"Isn't that what we've been doing? You said to wait until summertime, and here we are."

Marc sighed. "Look, one bedrooms start at twelve hundred a month, and that's not even within walking distance of campus. It's twice as much for anything closer in a halfway decent neighborhood. Unless you want to move back to that glorified broom closet you were living in before?"

"I don't mind paying the lion's share. We're in this together, right?"

"You've still got two years' worth of tuition to pay for. Let's just table it until I'm making more money at my writing. It won't kill us to stay here another year, or . . . well, whenever."

He'd been saying "whenever" a lot lately, ever since the night they'd argued about the DADT repeal. He'd been nervous and quiet by turns, which wasn't like him. He hadn't initiated sex either, which *really* wasn't like him. It was as if he were holding his breath, waiting for the other shoe to drop. Cole's heart ached to see him like this, but nothing he said or did seemed to reassure him.

After several silent minutes, Marc got up to rinse off his dishes. "Oh, I almost forgot. Your phone rang while you were out. Twice, in fact."

"Must be a wrong number. You're the only one who ever

calls me." Still, he rummaged in his backpack, pulled out his phone and flicked it on. His stomach hit the floor when he saw his parents' number on the missed-call list. Jesus. He hadn't talked to his mother since he'd moved in with Marc, probably because he'd shut off his landline at the same time. He'd given her his cell number ages ago, but she'd never used it. Until now, obviously.

"Oh, great," he muttered, punching the "call back" button. "She's gonna tear me a new one."

But when the line picked up, it wasn't her barking "H'lo?" in an all-too-familiar gravelly growl.

"Dad?" His first impulse was to hang up, but he couldn't. He'd gone numb from head to toe, Marc's bewildered, wide-eyed gaze reflecting his own right back at him. "What's wrong?"

"Aside from the fact that I've been waiting for you to return my calls for the past two hours?" An indignant breath, and then, "It's your mother. She took a bad fall this morning. She's in the hospital."

Oh, holy shit. "Is she okay?"

"She's got a concussion and a broken ankle. They're keeping her overnight for observation, but they think she'll be fine."

Relief washed over him so fast he had to grip the kitchen table to stay upright. "What happened?"

"She tumbled down the attic stairs. Good thing I was home at the time." A moment of awkward silence followed before he cleared his throat. "She hasn't seen or heard from you in a while, you know."

"Give me the hospital's number, and I'll call her tonight."

"So you can't be bothered to get on a fucking plane?"

It took Cole's last fiber of restraint to keep from snapping the old man's head off. Instead, he closed his eyes until the urge passed. "I'm not sure I can get away right now."

"What's the problem? It's the end of May, for Christ's sake.

Aren't your classes over with yet?" He let out an exasperated grunt, the same disapproving sound Cole had heard every day for the first eighteen years of his life. He could practically see his father's lips pressed into a hard, thin line, forehead scrunched up like a bulldog's. "Fine, then. Come or don't come, makes no goddamn difference to me. Your mother asked me to call. Now I can tell her I've done my duty."

The line clicked off.

Cole exhaled, smiling wanly when Marc came over to lay a hand on his arm. "You got the gist of that, huh?"

"All the important parts, anyway. Look, don't let me hold you back. If you need to go home, then go."

"Are you sure?"

"Don't be silly. It's your mom." Marc sat down again. "Don't you want to see her?"

"Her, yeah. Dad's another story. That phone convo was enough of a trial."

"Well, if you want me to come along for moral support, I can probably get a few days off. But I'll have to owe you for the airline ticket."

"I'd love it, but my folks wouldn't. Dad'll take one look at us and drop-kick both our asses out the front door." A hollow ache swelled inside him, his heart thumping double-time. "You're right, I'd better go. I'd never be able to live with myself if I didn't."

He got out his laptop to search for available flights. Leaving on such short notice would cost him a fortune no matter which airline he chose, so he opted for a 5 a.m. departure out of Oakland the next day. His father had evidently gone to bed already, so Cole left him a voicemail outlining all the pertinent details. Then he tossed some clothes and his shaving kit in his suitcase before sinking into bed, worn out at barely seven in the evening.

The edge of the mattress dipped, and Marc's arm snaked

around his waist, lips feathering warm, wet kisses down his chest. First time he'd put the moves on him in over a week. Within seconds, Cole was wide awake in every sense of the word.

They kissed and licked and sucked every naked inch of each other until he couldn't take any more. Fingers trembling, he managed to get himself sheathed and slicked, then kneed apart Marc's thighs and plunged inside him. A few desperate, stuttering thrusts was all either of them could stand. Cole tucked his face into the curve of Marc's throat as they shuddered and clung to each other, their cries loud enough to shake the walls.

"Jesus Christ," Cole muttered once he'd caught his breath. "I'm surprised our neighbors haven't called the cops."

Marc just smiled and snuggled closer, head pillowed on Cole's chest. It felt good. Right. The way things used to be. They'd had their first real fight, and they'd survived.

"Before I forget," Marc said, "make sure you write down the date and time of your return flight, so I can pick you up."

"I decided to leave it open-ended, just in case. Dad said Mama should be fine, but with head injuries you can never tell. There could be complications."

"Oh. I didn't think of that." Marc's smile faded. "So you might stay longer than a few days?"

"I don't know. But I'll call as soon as I do."

"Okay." He laid back down, swirling ticklish patterns on Cole's chest with his fingertips. "This is our first time being separated. Other than for work and school."

"You'll probably get so caught up in writing your next book you won't even notice I'm gone."

"I doubt it," Marc replied, and hugged him tighter.

CHAPTER 20

It was the trees Cole had missed the most. Huge, beautiful oaks and pines, the latter's sharp scent lingering in his nostrils. Oh, Berkeley had trees too—and flowers and bushes—tucked in neatly-groomed pockets of foliage that kept the endless streets and ugly concrete buildings plastered with tattered ads and handbills from being too fucking depressing. But he'd never seen green rolling hills like this anywhere in the Bay Area, or felt a sultry breeze practically reach out and grab him by the scruff of his neck. Ninety-something degrees with at least eighty percent humidity, though? That was one thing he hadn't missed.

The air whapped him in the face like a soggy blanket, his shirt sticking to him from the minute he stepped outside the terminal at Raleigh-Durham airport. And there stood his father, leaning against the back bumper of his ten-year-old Lincoln Continental, a cigarette between his teeth. He still sported the traditional Marine Corps haircut and wore his spotless khaki chinos and short-sleeved white cotton shirt as if it were his old uniform. Looked in fairly good shape for a guy pushing sixty, despite a few extra pounds around the belt. The semi-nauseating aroma of unfiltered tobacco and Old Spice drifted in Cole's direction as he walked up to the curb. At first he wasn't sure whether he should hold out his hand, but sheer nerves finally prompted him into it.

"Good to see you, sir." Not that he really meant it, but what the hell else was he supposed to say? *Thanks for dragging me away from my boyfriend* probably wouldn't go over too well.

"Who're you calling 'sir'? You're the officer in the family.

Oh, sorry. That's past tense, isn't it?" He tamped out his half-smoked Lucky Strike with the sole of his boot, then popped open the trunk. "Stow your crap and get in. Your mother's waiting to see you."

That was their first and last exchange the entire ride home. Finally they swung down a pleasant, tranquil street in North Ridge, and Cole's heart thumped when he caught sight of a familiar two-story white frame house perched primly on the next corner. His father turned into the wide driveway and let him out in front.

Cole had spent most of his summers and Christmases here as a child, back when it was his grandparents' house, and standing in its welcoming shadow never failed to put a smile on his face. But it quickly faded as he strode up to the porch. The lawn was shaggy and unkempt, with brown spots and even a few dandelions poking through. His mother's camellias drooped in the heat, plainly in need of a good watering.

What the fuck? The front yard was his parents' pride and joy. They used to be out here every weekend, fussing and trimming, making sure everything looked perfect. He and his mother always joked about his father cutting the lawn with fingernail scissors. He'd need a weed-whacker and a machete now.

Cole climbed the steps to the screened-in front porch and headed inside, blinking in the sudden gloom. The blinds were closed, as usual during sweltering summer afternoons, to help the central air keep everything cool. The muffled thump of someone else's footsteps drew him down the hallway to the kitchen, his own sneakers making a rubbery squeak on the hardwood floor.

A woman stood over the sink, but it wasn't his mother. Long blonde hair pulled back in a neat ponytail, pink blouse, jeans and flip-flops.

"I'd know the back of that head anywhere," he said with a grin.

"Cole! It's good to have you home." Jen set down the plate she'd been drying, her sweet face lighting up with a smile. Still as pretty as when they'd dated back in high school, pink-cheeked and glowing without a trace of makeup. But it wasn't until she came over to throw her arms around him that he noticed a bulge under her blouse. "Yup, I've got another one on the way," she added. "Obviously."

"Geez, Jen, you're gonna need to start your own baseball team pretty soon."

"Not hardly. Three is more than enough, thank you very much. Of course, that's what Lyle and I said after our second. Not that I mind; I enjoy being a mom. That is, when the little monsters aren't jumping on the bed waking me up every morning."

"My cat does the same thing." They both laughed. Jen's was soothing, natural and unforced. The sound of someone truly happy with her life. For the first time in his own life, Cole knew how she felt. "Don't take this the wrong way," he said, "but what're you doing here?"

"Oh, your daddy asked me to look in on your mama while he went to pick you up. She's still getting used to that cast they put on her ankle. And she didn't get much rest last night, what with the nurse waking her up every couple of hours. She's been sleeping off and on ever since he brought her home this morning."

As if on cue, his father came barreling through the kitchen door with a three-gallon jug of bottled water in one hand, Cole's suitcase in the other. His face was so red Cole was surprised he hadn't set off the fucking smoke alarm. Huffing and puffing, rivers of sweat pouring down his face, he put the water in the fridge, then headed for the stairs. But when Cole dashed after him and offered to carry the suitcase, his father yanked it out of his grasp.

"I'm not so old I can't tote a damn bag upstairs," he snapped. And with that, he continued on his way, apparent heat stroke be damned.

Jen flashed Cole a brittle smile as he ambled back into the kitchen. "I should get going. My boys are probably driving the sitter insane by now."

"Thanks for coming over. I appreciate it, and I'm sure Dad and Mama do, too."

"Oh, it's no problem. That's what friends do for each other, right?" Levering herself up on her tiptoes, she gave him a peck on the cheek. "If you need anything, my number's on the fridge."

He walked her to the front door, watching as she climbed into a dark blue SUV parked across the street. Then he went upstairs to check on his mother.

She was still asleep, lying on her back with her face turned away from him and the covers pulled up to her chin. The master bedroom faced east, so with the blinds shut and air conditioning on, it was actually a bit chilly. His father came out of the master bath, pressing a damp washcloth to the nape of his neck. His face still gleamed with moisture, though it was slightly less red than before. "I'd like to go stretch out on the couch for a bit," he said. "Would you mind sitting with her?"

Finally, a halfway civil tone—now that he wanted something. And of course, no apology for his earlier behavior, not that Cole expected one. "You want me to come get you when she wakes up?"

"Actually, you should wake her yourself in another hour or so. The doctor said she didn't think there was anything to worry about, but it can't hurt to be sure." His gaze landed on the bed, steely gray tinged with a distinctly sad undertone. Shoulders slumped, he trudged from the room, his footsteps dragging on the stairs. Not terribly surprising, considering how exhausted he looked. He'd be back to his ornery old self once he got some rest.

Cole sank down gratefully onto the armchair near the window. He needed to give Marc a call, but Marc was probably still at work. He'd do it after supper. Only a couple more hours.

He slouched against the backrest and started to drift, until his mother's soft moan jerked him back to reality. He sprang to his feet and was at her bedside in a split-second. "It's okay, Mama. I'm here."

She brushed back a stray lock of grayish-brown hair and levered herself up on one elbow, blinking groggily. For a few seconds, it seemed she didn't recognize him, but at last realization dawned. "Oh, Cole. It's good to see you, sweetheart." She pulled him into her arms and held him tight, her ribs poking his chest. Felt like she'd lost at least ten pounds since they'd last seen each other. "I didn't think you were coming."

"What, you mean Dad didn't tell you?"

"I'm sure he did, but this old noggin of mine's full of scrambled eggs. The last couple days are still a bit fuzzy." She let out a nervous chuckle and grabbed another pillow, making a pile to settle back on. "Well, tell me what you've been doing since the last time we talked."

There was a lot to tell, but he condensed it into bullet points. School. Therapy. Marc. He wasn't sure how she'd handle the news that he'd found a partner, never mind them moving in together. She took her time digesting it before nodding. "I'm happy for you. The notion of you spending your whole life alone never sat well with me. I still don't quite understand why you feel the way you do, but . . ."

"I love Marc, and he loves me. It's no different from the way you and Dad love each other. It means the same thing."

"He sounds like a very nice young man. But you probably shouldn't mention him to your father unless you want another argument on your hands."

They talked for a while longer, then Cole helped her on with her robe and tucked her arm in his as they maneuvered down the stairs to the living room. His father was awake, sitting on the couch reading the paper. There were newspapers and magazines everywhere, in fact, overflowing the oak stand beside the couch and piled haphazardly on the coffee table, which wore a thin film of dust. Crumbs and other pale specks of dirt littered the navy blue carpet. The room had been so dark before, Cole hadn't noticed it. It struck him as odd, to say the least. His mother usually kept an exceptionally tidy house.

"Oh my." Twin spots of bright pink appeared high on her cheeks. "Could've sworn I straightened up in here just the other day."

"It's okay, Mama. Don't worry about it." He led her over to the recliner and waited for her to get settled, then gathered up all the old papers and carried them out to the trash. His stomach growled as he walked back to the house. Aside from a half-stale ham sandwich and a couple packets of peanuts on the plane, he hadn't eaten a thing all day. He opened the fridge to discover it empty except for the jug of water and a carton of leftover chow mein on the verge of going bad. There were a few cans of soup in the cupboard above the stove, but it was too fucking hot for that.

His father showed up at the doorway, fists planted on his hips. "What're you poking around in here for?"

"When was the last time you bought groceries?"

"I think Jennifer brought us some last week. Or maybe it was the week before."

Jesus. He didn't even want to think about what that meant. Not right now, anyway. "Give me the car keys," Cole said, holding out his hand. "Unless you want ice cubes for dinner."

His father glanced down at the floor for a moment, then forked them over. "Get some strawberry yogurt. Your mother likes it for breakfast."

The nearest market was in a strip mall a few miles away. Close to dinner time, it was already pretty packed. But that didn't stop people he'd never met from holding the door for him, or smiling and saying hello as he pushed his cart up and down the aisles. He'd missed this friendliness and sense of community. People in Berkeley didn't even make eye contact half the time.

He bought enough food for the next few days, including a Caesar salad from the deli, then headed back, put everything away, and set the kitchen table, just like he'd gotten into the habit of doing at home. God, how he wished he could just snap his fingers and be magically teleported to their cramped little apartment, Marc typing away in the living room and Thomas curled up at his feet while he studied. Instead, he tossed the salad, filled three plates, and called his parents in to eat.

Salad wasn't his father's favorite meal, but despite his initial grumbling, he polished off two helpings. Mama picked at her food, claiming she still had a headache. They chatted about inane things like the weather and Jen's family while his father stared out the window. Still, it was a much more pleasant dinner than the last one they'd shared at this table ten months ago. Cole concentrated on enjoying it, and brushed aside the thousand or so questions niggling at the back of his mind.

The second I sat down at my desk to work, my phone rang, and I dove for it when I saw Cole's number flashing on the display. "Hey. I was getting worried. I already left you a couple messages."

"Yeah, I just noticed. Sorry. I've barely had a chance to catch my breath all day, much less make a phone call." He huffed as if he'd just set down a fifty-pound boulder. "My folks hit the sack at the stroke of nine. It's a wild life we lead here in North Carolina."

"Is everything okay?"

Another sigh. "To be honest, I don't know."

I tensed, my hand gripping the phone. "Tell me."

"The house is a fucking mess, Mama's confused, and Dad's not talking. But it's the first part that makes the rest twice as alarming. Normally Mama would never let the place get to such a state."

"You think there's something else wrong with her besides the concussion?"

"That's what I've been wondering. I mean, this didn't all happen overnight. I'll see if I can corner my father tomorrow and get some answers out of him. That should be tons of fun."

He sounded so stressed and frustrated, I wanted wrap him in my arms from three thousand miles away. "Why don't you go for a run? That usually helps you unwind."

"I will once it cools down a bit. Might be the only way I get to sleep. I packed in such a hurry, I forgot my meds."

"I know. I found them on the bathroom counter when I got back from dropping you at the airport. Thought about running them out to you, but I figured skipping a few days probably wouldn't hurt."

"Would you mind putting them in the mail? The way things are going here, I've got a feeling I'll need them."

"Oh." My stomach tightened. "You really think you'll be gone that long?"

"No idea, but at this point I'd best prepare myself for anything."

Thomas came over and jumped into my lap, butting his head against the phone as if he knew who I was talking to. "Well, get home as soon as you can. I miss you, and so does a certain fur-person who's been pining by the door ever since you left."

He laughed, and it was the best damn thing I'd heard all day. "God, I love you."

Okay, second best. "I love you too. I'll get the pills in the mail tomorrow."

"Thanks. Talk to you soon."

I clicked off the phone and tossed it back on the desk. "Looks like it's just you and me here for a while, Thomas."

With a tiny squeak, he sprang up, scampered over to the door again and planted himself in front of it. I was sorely tempted to join him.

CHAPTER 21

Cole found his dress blues hanging at the back of the guest room closet, still in plastic from their last dry cleaning. He didn't know why the hell his mother had kept them when he'd told her to give all his old clothes to charity before he'd left for Berkeley. The last time he'd worn them was at his best friend Ian's wedding. Eight months later, Ian had taken a gutful of shrapnel at Fallujah and bled out all over the sand. Squeezing his eyes shut, Cole closed the closet door and headed down to the kitchen.

His parents were sitting at the table, drinking coffee and reading the paper. Mama had a small bowl of yogurt in front of her, while his father nibbled on dry toast. No eggs or sausage, which was what his mother had fixed for breakfast every morning since he was a kid. But after all, she was still recovering. He wouldn't want to stand over a hot stove with a fiberglass cast on his foot, either.

He poured himself some coffee and sat down. His father stood at practically the same moment, shoved his hands in his pockets and stalked off to the living room. So much for conversation—not that Cole could quiz him about his mother with her sitting right there. Naturally, she ignored the latest elephant in the room and started chatting blithely about her friends at church.

Things carried on in the same strained manner for the next few days. Cole spent his time cleaning up the house and visiting with his mother when she wasn't resting. The fall had taken a lot out of her. She was pretty badly bruised and still experiencing periods of disorientation. Sometimes she'd trail off in the middle of a sentence, or cast a momentarily panicked glance around the room. She didn't cook at all anymore. In fact, she gave their gas stove a wide berth, as if she were afraid it'd bite her. One night he woke up to find her roaming up and down the hallway searching for the bathroom. In all his years on active duty, Cole had seen plenty of fellow Marines with concussions, and this was *not* fucking normal.

One evening after he'd finished his run, Cole plodded back to the house to find his father in the garage, tinkering with his old '65 Mustang. Perfect opportunity for a little talk.

His father straightened up, back going ramrod stiff as Cole approached. "I don't need any help."

"Who says I'm offering?" Here came the silent treatment again. Well, fuck that. "What's the matter with Mama? She should be getting better by now."

"I don't know what you're talking about."

"The hell you don't. She was fine when I left last summer, so what happened?"

His father looked up from fiddling with the distributor cap, wiping his hands on a rag tucked into his belt. "She wasn't fine," he replied at last, in the weariest tone Cole had ever heard him use. "She hasn't been fine for a while. Only difference is, now she can't cover it up anymore."

"She's fifty-five. That's too young to be going senile."

"It's early-onset Alzheimer's. I finally got her to the doctor for a diagnosis last fall."

Cole stared at him, suddenly so shaky he had to drop onto a nearby stool. "Y-you've known for months, and you didn't bother to *tell* me?"

"There's nothing you could've done all the way out in California."

A bullshit excuse, but Cole didn't have the heart to call him on it. "I can't believe I never noticed any signs before now."

"She has good days and bad days. She made sure you only

saw or talked to her on the good ones. She had me fooled for a long time too. A year ago last spring, she got lost on her way to the market. Left the car at the side of the road and started wandering into traffic. The police found her and brought her home. She hasn't left the house by herself since."

"And you let her go up to the attic by herself?"

"I didn't *let* her do anything. I can't keep my eye on her twenty-four seven, for Christ's sake!"

Cole swallowed hard. "Is that why you retired last year?" he asked, realizing the truth of it even as he said it. "I thought you'd planned to wait 'til you turned sixty."

His father gave a hesitant nod. "That, and my high blood pressure. Which you've probably already figured out."

Not in so many words, but it certainly explained why he couldn't handle the heat anymore. "Have you looked into getting some help?"

"Jennifer and a couple other ladies from church drop by every now and then to bring groceries and tidy up the house. They've been the soul of discretion. Last thing we need is everyone gossiping about us."

Of course. Because talking about unpleasant things was worse than them happening in the first place. "What I meant was getting some help with Mama, so you can take a break."

Cole's father stiffened again, his mouth going tight. "I don't need any help. I'm fine."

"Dad, you can't keep this up indefinitely. You want to end up with a stroke or a heart attack from all the stress?"

"I always thought I'd go first. Hell, I've been wounded enough times," his father said quietly. "Never dreamed I'd have to stand idly by and watch her slip away by slow degrees. But we've been married thirty-two years. I'm not about to give her over to the care of strangers, not yet. Not until I've got no other choice. And that's final."

Cole tried to sleep, but even with his medication, he tossed and turned for hours. He finally dropped off a little after oh-two-hundred, but soon awoke with a jolt, his heart pounding, sounds and images of Fallujah racing through his brain. His first nightmare in months. He flailed out instinctively, reaching for Marc. Took him a minute to realize Marc wasn't there.

He grabbed his phone off the bedside table and hit the speed-dial.

Marc's groggy voice echoed over the line. "Cole? You okay?"

"Define okay."

"That sounds ominous." A soft rustle of bed covers, then, "What's going on?"

Cole gave him the quick thumbnail version, followed by a long silence. "I'm sorry," Marc murmured at last. "Don't know what else to say."

"Just hearing your voice is enough. I still wish you were here, though."

"So do I, but you seem to be handling it pretty well, considering. Can't say the same for your dad."

"Now I know how you feel when you bitch about my control-freak tendencies." That made them both chuckle.

"What're you planning to do?" Marc asked.

"I have no fucking clue. Mama needs more help than Dad can give her, but he just keeps burying his head in the sand. She could've gotten killed falling down those stairs. How much more of a wake-up call does he need?" He rubbed his eyes. "Maybe I should talk to Jen. She's always been pretty wise about this kind of stuff."

"Jen, your ex? You didn't tell me you'd reconnected with your old sweetheart," Marc teased.

"Oh, stop. She's happily married with two kids and another on the way. Besides, we've always been more like brother and sister than anything else."

"Just make sure you keep it that way."

"You're cute," Cole retorted, and hung up with a grin.

Jen's two boys looked just like her, a pair of apple-cheeked tow-heads laughing and running through the sprinkler on their front lawn. Cole watched them wistfully, remembering familiar happy times from his own childhood. He and Marc had never talked about having kids. Maybe in a few years, once he was out of school and Marc started making decent money with his writing.

Jen greeted him at the front door and ushered him inside. It was a lot smaller than his parents' place, a single-story fixer-upper with living room walls painted a bright, cheery yellow, toys strewn all over the furniture.

"I'd apologize for the mess, but it pretty much always looks like this," she said, leading him into the kitchen. "Have a seat and I'll get us some tea."

Sweet tea with a slice of lemon and plenty of ice—his favorite drink on a blazing hot day. "So when are you due?" he asked as she flicked on the oscillating fan and sat down. It kept the air moving, but didn't really cool things off. Cole could already feel sweat beading up on his forehead and the nape of his neck. "I can't believe you don't have central air. You must be miserable."

"I swear, Lyle and I have the worst timing ever. Both our boys were born during the dog days of summer. I've got six more weeks to go on this one, give or take." She picked up the morning paper and began fanning herself. "Much as I hate saying so, I doubt I'll be able to keep helping out your folks once this baby comes."

Cole forced a smile. "Don't apologize. You've already gone above and beyond. They'd be up a creek without you and the other church ladies."

"I love your mama and daddy like my own parents, you know that. And I've tried talking to him about bringing in professional help, but he won't hear of it. He's afraid she'll think he doesn't love her anymore. He spent so much time away from her when he was on active duty, he doesn't want to waste a single moment now. It's sad, but kind of sweet, too."

"You make him sound like an old romantic."

"Scratch a Marine, find a heart of gold. I learned that in high school," she replied with a wink.

"I wasn't a Marine in high school."

"Sure you were. You were practically born in fatigues."

He laughed. "Guess you always had me figured out, even back then."

"I knew you were different from most of the other guys at school. I mean, you never tried to pressure me. But it was frustrating, knowing our friends were all doing it, when you wouldn't go beyond kissing and hand-holding even after we got engaged." She scooped up her glass and pressed it against her flushed cheek. "Didn't realize how lucky I was being with someone who liked *me* instead of what I had in my pants, even if it took a few years before I understood why. Going to Duke instead of Bob Jones was the best decision I ever made, aside from marrying Lyle. Got me out of that sanitized fundamentalist bubble I was raised in and showed me there's a big, wide world out there with all kinds of wonderful people in it. It opened up my eyes to a lot of things."

"I never told you how much I appreciated you coming by to see me after I was discharged. It meant a lot."

"Of course. No matter what, I hope we'll always be friends." She reached for a pamphlet on the counter and handed it to him. "This is the home health care agency I talked to your daddy about. They're fully bonded, and they run background checks on all their employees. Their rates aren't too bad, either. Maybe you'll have better luck convincing him than I did."

Cole tucked it into his pocket, suppressing a sigh. "I've already tried, but I guess it's time for round two. Nothing like trying to push a rock up a mountain, right?"

His father picked up the sports section and strode right out of the kitchen when Cole tried to show him the pamphlet the next morning. Well, he wasn't about to be stonewalled this time. Marching up to the couch, he skewered his father with a determined glare. "We have to figure something out sooner or later."

His father folded back the paper, eyeballing the box scores. "Her ankle's healing just fine. As for the other, well, I don't see any reason to confuse her with unnecessary changes in her routine."

"So you'd rather take a header into your dinner plate like you nearly did last night? Dad, you're exhausted. You can't keep this up forever."

"I survived thirty years in the Corps. Losing a little sleep won't hurt me."

CHAPTER 22

I hadn't heard from Cole in two days. I'd left messages, sent texts, but he hadn't replied. Hopefully his mother hadn't taken a bad turn.

I hit the speed-dial again as I left the diner and started off home, my heart almost skidding to a halt when Cole's voice finally crackled over the line. "Oh, thank God! I was ready to start panicking. Why didn't you call me back?"

"Sorry. I turned my phone off for a while. I needed some time to think."

He sounded more wrung out than I'd ever heard him. "Is your mom okay?"

"As okay as she can be. Guess I just have to accept that it's all downhill from here."

"I'm sorry, I really am," I murmured, lame a response as it was. "But I wanted to let you know your registration packet for the fall semester came in the mail yesterday. Classes start in another month."

"That's actually what I've been thinking about. What would you say if I took a leave of absence this semester?"

I froze in the middle of the sidewalk. "You . . . you mean you're not coming back at *all*?"

"Just until I can persuade Dad to hire in-home care for Mama. After what he's told me about the last year and a half, I'm apprehensive about going off and leaving them. Health-wise, he's not doing so well himself."

"And there's no other alternative? Don't they have friends who can look in on them?"

"Sure they do, but they can't be here twenty-four seven."

"Does your mom need that kind of care already? I thought you said she'd only been diagnosed last year." My mind raced, but I forced myself to calm down. One of us had to remain rational. "Think about this, Cole. You sound ready to collapse. Can you really keep this up for another few months?"

"That's what I said to my dad the other day, for all the good it did." He sighed. "Look, I don't like this any more than you do, but I've mulled it over every which way, and I can't see any other solution. It's not the end of the world, okay? I'll try to visit for Thanksgiving; it is kind of our anniversary, after all. Or maybe you could . . ."

God, what was so awful he couldn't even finish his sentence? "Maybe I could what?"

"Maybe you could move out here with me, and I could transfer to the law school at Duke."

I had to stop and lean against the nearest building, a gust of wind blowing the ragged end of a club poster in my face. "You're joking, right?"

"Well, why not? Pack up your clothes and your laptop, put Thomas in a carrier, and get on a fucking plane. You can write anywhere, can't you?"

"I'm not exactly making Stephen King money yet. How the hell am I supposed to pay for rent and groceries without a day job?"

"Jesus, Marc, there are diners everywhere. Or maybe you could get an office job. At least that way we could keep similar hours."

Was he *kidding*? "I've worked in offices before. I fucking hated it. Besides, haven't you heard there's a recession going on? What if I move out there and I can't find any work at all?" *Or what if I move out there—where I don't know anyone but you—and we break up? What happens then?*

"One thing at a time, okay? Let's worry about getting you here first."

A slow, insistent throb blossomed behind my eyes. I couldn't believe we were discussing this as if it'd already been decided. "But what about your treatment? You've been doing so well."

"I can't think about that right now," he snapped. "My mother needs me."

"What about *my* mother? If I move back east, it could be years before I see her again. What if she gets sick while I'm stuck on the other side of the damn country?"

"She looked pretty healthy to me at Christmas."

"And I'm sure your mom seemed fine last summer, too."

His silence told me I'd struck a nerve. I bit my lip, wishing we could rewind this whole conversation and start over.

"Marc, c'mon. I'm getting pulled in five directions at once. Why are you making things even harder?"

I sank down heavily on a nearby bus stop bench. The older woman knitting there shot me a sharp look and scooted to the other end. "From what you've told me about your mom, she sounds like a pretty tough lady. I can't believe she'd want you to put your entire life on hold to take care of her."

"Somebody has to, and Dad's not dealing at all. I don't know what else to do. I'm afraid if I leave for a few months, she won't even recognize me when I come back."

His voice cracked, tearing right through me. He hadn't sounded so fearful and broken since the night he'd had that flashback in the alley. "I wish I could help. I wish I could be there with you right now. But—"

"But what?"

Go ahead, say it. Get it out in the open. "But my life is here, Cole. My family and friends are here. They're my support system. I can't leave them behind."

"Not even for me?" A sharp intake of breath, then, "Why don't you stop skating around the issue? You think I'm an idiot? You think I haven't figured out why you've been holding me at arm's length ever since I moved in? You're so convinced I'm going to dump you, it's almost like you're pushing me into it. Well, fine." Another breath. "It wouldn't be fair for me to ask you to wait indefinitely, so don't. Forget about me and get on with your life."

It hit me like a punch to the gut, nearly doubling me over. "So that's it? You're breaking up with me over the fucking *phone?*"

Just like Rob and Tony had done.

"I'm sorry. But we might as well get it over with. If you were in my shoes, I wouldn't blame you for doing the same thing." He huffed out a breath. "I'd better go."

The line disconnected, leaving me with an earful of dead air. My phone slipped from my fingers and bounced off the toe of my sneaker before hitting the sidewalk, a long, jagged crack bisecting the display. I couldn't be bothered to care.

CHAPTER 23

I thought about calling in sick to the diner the next morning, but with Cole gone, I couldn't afford to pass up a day's pay. I wandered around the place in a daze, serving up orders on autopilot. Nothing seemed real. How could it, when my whole world had just been shattered?

Terry finally cornered me in the kitchen when I went back to pick up a couple of omelets. "What's the matter?" she asked. "You've barely said a dozen words all morning."

"Nothing," I snapped. "Except my life fucking *sucks*."

"Whoa, what brought this on all of a sudden? Trouble in paradise?"

"You could say that." I didn't want to elaborate, but she'd just keep poking at me until I caved. "Long story short—Cole's not coming home. *Ever*." I scooped up my plates and tried to brush past her, but she grabbed my arm. "Terry, c'mon—"

"Oh no you don't. You can't drop a bombshell like that and just walk away. There's got to be more to it, so spill."

I gave her the condensed version, though by the time I'd reached the end it really was spilling out of me, word after word until I'd let it all loose at last. Still didn't make me feel any better. In fact, now I had this empty ache in my stomach, as if I hadn't eaten in days. "I told him he was out of his mind, but he wouldn't listen to me."

"He's not the only one."

"What's that supposed to mean?"

Terry yanked the plates out of my hands, setting them back under the warming lamps. "Do you love this guy, or don't you?"

"It's not that simple."

"Sure it is. And if the answer's still yes, you need to pack your crap and get your cute little buns on a plane."

I snorted. "Oh, so I should just pull up stakes and move to North Carolina with no guarantee any of this is gonna work out?"

"Who said anything about guarantees? Sure, it's a gamble—a pretty big one, in fact. But don't you think he's worth it?"

She wasn't telling me anything I hadn't told myself a thousand times since I'd talked to Cole yesterday. But I still didn't want to listen. "You don't get it."

"Oh, I think I do. You want Cole, but you don't want to sacrifice anything for him. Well, that's not the way relationships work, kiddo, and I've got two broken marriages and God knows how many ex-boyfriends to prove it. You used to have your head on straight where this stuff was concerned, so you need to sit yourself down and figure out what's really important here. If you're not willing to budge, then you deserve to lose him."

Our conversation buzzed around in my head for the rest of the day, nagging at me even after I got home. My latest royalty check had come in the mail, my eyes bulging when I saw it—enough to cover my rent and buy a few groceries besides. I fed Thomas, then sat down to work, but it was like trying to pull every word out of my brain with fucking pliers. Finally I shut my laptop, yanked off my glasses, and rested my head on my folded arms.

My eyes burned, but I was too damn exhausted to cry. The quiet had never bothered me before, but now I missed hearing Cole putter around in the kitchen, studying at the table. The occasional rustle as he turned a page. His happy chuckle when Thomas jumped in his lap.

All these things I'd taken for granted, and now the loss of

them sliced through me so sharply it left me shaking. I'd had the kind of love most people would kill for, and I'd let it go. Hell, I'd practically shoved it away. How could I have been so fucking *stupid?*

Stupid, blind, and *selfish*. Terry was right—I didn't want to make sacrifices, even when I'd pushed Cole to make so many of his own. Any other guy would've walked out on me a long time ago. Which was, of course, exactly what that little voice at the back of my mind had been hoping for—because it let me off the hook.

I lifted my head and raked my hair out of my eyes, blinking hazily at the empty room. My gaze settled on Cole's textbooks, waiting to be sold back to the campus bookstore. They never would be. I'd never hear him traipse through the front door again. Never get up with him again at five in the fucking morning to hit the gym.

He'd told me to forget him, but how could I? Everywhere I looked, I saw him. His gentle drawl still echoed inside my head. I couldn't just climb out of bed tomorrow and carry on as if he'd never been here.

I opened my laptop and started searching for flights to Raleigh, my fingers trembling on the keys. It was crazy, going all the way out there with no guarantee Cole would even talk to me.

Well, fuck guarantees. If there was even the tiniest chance, I had to try.

Cole's mother appeared in the kitchen doorway in her Sunday best—a prim, pretty blue dress with matching low-heeled pumps—tucking a packet of tissues into her purse. "Are you sure you don't want to come along with us to church?" she asked. "There're plenty of people who'd be glad to see you."

She was always so damn optimistic, so willing to believe the best of people. Sadly, Cole knew better. No way was he about to put on a suit and go sit among those same pious hypocrites who'd snubbed him after his discharge. "Not today, Mama. I'm kind of tired."

"I can see that." She came over and laid a hand on his shoulder. "You've been so quiet these past few days. Anything you'd like to tell me?"

Fresh pain welled at the memory of his last conversation with Marc. While he would've loved to confide in her—longed for it, in fact—what good would it do? Nothing either of them said or did would fix it. "No reason to concern yourself. I'm fine."

"Oh, stop fibbing. You think I can't tell when my boy's upset?"

He laughed. It'd been so long since the last time, his chest ached. "Your *boy?* Geez, Mama, I'm thirty years old!"

"I don't care if you're eighty and in a wheelchair, you'll always be my boy. You don't have to—" The beep of the Continental's horn cut her off. She gave his father a quick wave through the kitchen window before planting a kiss on Cole's cheek. "What I meant to say is, whatever's troubling you, you don't have to carry it on your own."

"I wish there was an alternative."

"There is, you know. Why don't you just call him?"

Cole's reply caught in his throat. Then the front door opened and in marched his father, dressed in his lightweight gray summer suit, face already red from just a few minutes outside. "For Heaven's sake, Livvy, stop dawdling or we'll be late. I don't want to end up standing through the entire service in this heat."

Her face went blank, the way it did at random unexpected moments, her gaze flicking from Cole to his father, then down at herself, as if she didn't recognize her own body. Cole jumped up to help steady her, but the lapse passed as quickly as it had come. "Oh, of course," she said with a shaky smile, taking his father's hand. "Sorry to keep you waiting, dear."

Cole watched through the window as they climbed into the car and drove away, blissful silence descending at last, broken only by the low hum of the central air unit. After a few minutes, though, it felt more eerie than blissful. He never used to mind being left alone with his thoughts, but right now that was the last thing he wanted. Maybe he'd take a walk to that nice, shady pond a short stretch down the road. Might help clear his head.

He'd just carried his breakfast dishes over to the sink when the doorbell buzzed. For a second he considered ignoring it. The only people who ever came around uninvited were evangelical types or kids selling magazines, and he wasn't in the mood to deal with either. Oh, wait—it was probably Jen. She'd left her sunglasses behind the other day. They were still sitting on the counter.

He grabbed them and made a beeline for the door. "I was wondering when you were coming back for—" He swung the door open, and his whole world shimmied before his eyes. "Wh— What the hell are you doing here?"

"Good to see you, too," Marc replied. His t-shirt was all wrinkled, as if he'd slept in it, although the dark circles under his eyes told a different story. Then he smiled, and the floor dropped out from under Cole's feet. "Mind if I come in?"

Cole gaped at me as if he thought I'd disappear in a puff of smoke—which seemed weirdly apropos, considering I'd been fucking *roasting* ever since I'd stumbled off the damn plane. "Okay, fine. I'll just melt to death here on your front porch."

At last he stepped aside to let me in. I stifled a grateful

groan at the first kiss of cool air wafting over my skin. Jesus, how did people *live* in this humidity?

"You still haven't answered my question," Cole said. He wore this strange expression—stunned, angry, even a bit freaked out. I couldn't really blame him.

"I just wanted to—" My voice cracked, a nagging little tickle at the back of my throat. "Um, sorry. Can I have a glass of water?"

He turned and led me into the kitchen. It was brighter in here, sunshine pouring through the curtains. Pleasant and homey. Reminded me of my mom's kitchen. Cole gestured for me to take a seat at the table, then filled a glass from the tap and handed it to me. I hoped he'd sit down too, but instead he leaned against the counter, gaze dropping to the floor, mouth going tight.

I downed half the water in one long gulp and wiped my mouth with the back of my hand. "Thanks." He still didn't reply, or even look at me. It wasn't as if I'd expected a ticker-tape parade, but Christ, couldn't he at least give me a little eye contact? "Look, all I want is to clear the air. After the way we left things—"

"Oh, you're fucking kidding me." He sent me a glare—a pretty damn murderous one. "You flew three thousand miles just to *talk*? What's wrong with the damn telephone?"

"If I'd called, would you have picked up?"

His lips twitched. "What exactly do you want to talk about? Seems to me you made yourself perfectly clear the other day."

"I know that's how it sounded, but I was wrong. I was a selfish asshole, and I'm sorry. I don't want us to break up." Deep breath. "I love you, and I'm willing to do whatever's necessary so we can stay together. Even move here."

For a moment Cole remained completely still, then he yanked out the chair opposite me and crumpled onto it. I slid my hand across the table, but the second our fingers touched, I heard the crunch of tires on gravel. A door slammed, and then someone shouted, "Cole, get out here! We need some help!"

"Shit." Cole sprang to his feet, bolted for the back door and dashed outside. I couldn't see what was going on from where I was sitting, but it sounded pretty fucking intense—two deep male voices trying to soothe a woman whose shaky tone was skirting the edge of hysteria.

At last they managed to calm her enough to get her into the house. She looked so tiny sandwiched between them, terrified and utterly wrecked. I immediately rose, intending to offer my help, until I realized that would probably just panic her more. So I sat back down, holding my breath as Cole and his father led her upstairs, and sent up a silent prayer that she wouldn't notice me and go off again. Luckily, both she and Cole's father were too distracted to glance in my direction.

I wiped my clammy hands on my jeans and got up to put my glass in the sink. Maybe I should go. Cole obviously didn't need to deal with me right now on top of everything else.

I spied a scratch pad on the counter and started to write him a note, but then I heard the thump of familiar footsteps on the stairs, and in he came, pale and plainly upset. "Sorry you had to see that."

Jesus, why the hell was he apologizing? "What happened?"

"She asked my dad to take her to church today. First time she's felt up to it since she got home from the hospital. She had a little episode before they left, but after that she seemed fine. But once they got there, she didn't recognize where she was, and she just freaked." He flipped on the faucet to splash some cool water on his face and neck, then blotted his skin with a paper towel. "Dad's giving her a tranquilizer. Hopefully she'll sleep for the rest of the afternoon."

I didn't know what else to say, so I wrapped my arms around him, hands sliding up his back. Cole sucked in a long, shuddery breath and buried his face in my throat. "God, I've missed you," he whispered. "I still can't believe you flew all this way to—"

"Well, I did, and I'm glad." Four and a half hours in a cramped, stuffy plane, wedged in beside a stressed-out mother and her screaming baby, and it was all worth it just for this moment. "Are you?"

He lifted his head, the huge smile spreading across his lips telling me all I needed to know. At long fucking *last*, he leaned in for a kiss—

"What the hell's going on here?" Jerking apart, we swung around to find his father looming in the doorway, fists planted on his hips. His narrowed gaze ping-ponged from me to Cole and back again. "Who's this?"

Cole shot me a "Should I?" look, and after a second's hesitation, I nodded. After what his father had just walked in on, there was no point in denying it. "Dad, this is Marc," he said. "My partner."

"Your *what?*"

"We live together in California."

His jaw dropped, and his already flushed face went damn near purple as his eyes locked on me. "You've got some nerve coming into my house, you little queer. Get out of here before I boot your pansy ass into the next county."

Cole launched himself at his father, snapping, "Don't you fucking talk to him like that!" I had to grab his arm to pull him back. "Apologize!"

"Like hell I will!"

"It's okay," I said to Cole. "I'll go." I let go of his arm and made for the back door, which still yawned open. "I don't want to cause any trouble."

My shitty economy rental car was parked at the curb. Cole ran after me, catching up just as I opened the driver's side door. "I'm sorry," he said. "I could strangle him for—"

"Shut up." I looped an arm around his waist and levered myself up for that kiss he owed me. Our first in nearly two months. God, I'd forgotten how good he tasted, so clean and sweet. I swayed on my feet, half from him, half from the awful heat, half from sheer exhaustion.

Lack of air finally forced us apart. "I've been up since two-thirty this morning, California time," I murmured. "I'm gonna keel over if I don't get some rest."

"Where are you staying?"

"That motel down the road. The Live Oak Inn."

"What's your room number?"

I grinned. "109. But give me a few hours, all right? Unless you want me to conk out on you."

"Like I care." He grinned back. "I'll come by after dinner."

Cole knocked on room 109 around nineteen hundred with some leftover Caesar salad and a bottle of red wine. His stomach did this euphoric little flip-flop when Marc opened the door in nothing but his pajama pants, his hair all mussed from bed. "I, uh," Cole said, "I thought you might be hungry."

Marc yanked him inside and shut the door, then reached for Cole's belt. "I'm starving."

Cole let Marc strip him out of his clothes and push him back on the rumpled bed, eyes drifting shut, relishing the feel of Marc's lips and fingertips kissing, licking, touching him *everywhere*. Didn't take long before his cock began to throb, though he tried to ignore it. Tonight he didn't care if he came. He didn't even care if they fucked. All he wanted was to be close to Marc again, feel his warmth and taste the salt on his skin. To be reminded he wasn't alone, at least for now.

Then Marc slipped a pair of fingers in Cole's mouth and whispered, "Suck me," and suddenly coming seemed like a really, *really* good idea. Cole bit back a whimper as Marc grabbed both their cocks in his spit-slicked palm and started stroking. Too hot, too good. Too damn fast, with him too far gone to care. He twisted his hands in the covers and held on until Marc gave this exquisite, broken little gasp and spurted over his own fist. Cole followed a few seconds later, black spots dancing before his eyes.

"Well," he panted, "that was different."

Marc gave him a long, leisurely kiss that didn't do a damn thing to slow his pulse, then grabbed some tissues from the bedside table to wipe them both off. "Not bad for improvising, huh? Didn't realize 'til after we'd started that I forgot to bring supplies."

Cole remembered that night on his couch during the power failure and started to laugh. "So you weren't planning to jump my bones? Not sure if I should be flattered or insulted."

"Neither. I just packed in a hurry."

Ravenous again even though he'd just had dinner, he helped Marc dig into the salad. They ended up drinking the wine straight from the bottle, not that either of them cared. They'd never shared a meal in bed before. He could definitely get used to it.

"So I was thinking," Marc said, taking another swig from the bottle, "it'll probably take me about a month to get rid of all the stuff I'm not bringing with me. Guess there's no point shipping the furniture—we'll just buy new stuff once we get a place."

God, Marc was really serious about this? Hell, he could hardly believe Marc was actually here. Any second he expected to open his eyes and find himself alone in his parents' guest room. "I hope you've given this plenty of thought."

"You think I'd fly all the way out here if I wasn't prepared to go through with it? I told you, I'm willing to do whatever's necessary for us to be together."

"And if you'd said that on the phone the other day, I would've been fucking ecstatic. But now . . ." He sat up straight, shaking his head. What the hell had he been thinking, inviting Marc to move out here with him? It was way too much to ask of anyone, even under normal circumstances. "This thing with my mom's not easy to deal with. She can be perfectly fine one minute, and the next, she's like a total stranger."

"What, you don't think I can handle it?"

"There are days when *I* can barely handle it, and I *have* to. You don't." He exhaled. "As for my dad . . ."

"He was pretty upset about your mom. Cut him some slack. I'm sure he'll come around eventually."

"You don't know him the way I do. Half the time he treats me like I'm dipped in shit."

"Well, he'll have to change his tune once I start dropping by to help every day."

"Marc, you don't get it," Cole said slowly. "He's an old-school Marine with a very set way of looking at the world. Everything's either black or white to him. Right or wrong. If he won't even accept his own son, what makes you think he'll accept you?"

Marc stared at him, swallowing another sip of wine. He couldn't have looked more stunned if Cole had hauled off and slapped him.

"Look, as much as I appreciate your offer, I think moving here would be a big mistake." Scratch that—*now* Marc couldn't have looked more stunned. Cole scooped up his hand, cradling it between both of his. "Sooner or later you'll start resenting me for making you leave your friends and your job and your mom behind. I love you, Marc, and I want you to be happy. But believe me, you'll be miserable here. *I* don't even want to be here. I'd give my left nut to get on a plane back to California with you tomorrow."

"Why don't we leave your left nut where it is, okay?" There was that crooked smile he loved so much, and Marc's comforting arms wrapped around him, pulling him back down beside him. "I like knowing where I can find it. And all your other parts, too."

He carded his fingers through Marc's dark curls, inhaling the faint piney scent of his shampoo. "Go home and take care of Thomas. I'll be back to see you when I can."

"Still think it'll be a few months?"

"Honestly, I have no idea. But I've got a feeling we should get ready for the long haul."

"All right." Marc sighed.

They lay there in silence for a while. Eventually, reluctantly, Cole rolled to his feet and got dressed.

"You're welcome to stay if you want," Marc murmured.

No, he couldn't. If he didn't walk out of here now, he never would. "Better not. I should get the car back, just in case."

Marc's sad, sympathetic nod nearly broke him in half. "Sure."

"But hey, I'm taking my mom to the doctor's in the morning. Maybe we could meet for coffee after, if she feels up to it?"

"All right," Marc said again.

He planted a soft kiss on Marc's lips and headed out the door, steeling himself not to look back. Jesus, why couldn't he figure out a way to fix this?

He drove the five miles back to his parents' house as slowly as he could without making every other car on the road blast their horns. He let himself in through the back door and crept upstairs, wincing at every creak and groan in the floorboards. Thirty years old and here he was, sneaking into his room like some guilty teenager after curfew. What the fuck was he so afraid of—his father's hard stare and stony silence over breakfast tomorrow? Wasn't like it'd be any different from any other morning.

To hell with that. He'd had his fill of being treated like a fucking criminal.

Cole escorted his mother into the motel's tiny coffee shop and brought her over to the quiet corner booth where I was sitting. He looked a bit apprehensive—well, okay, a *lot* apprehensive—as he introduced us, though her warm, sincere smile put me immediately as ease. Evidently, Raleigh was a pretty small town, because she greeted our waitress by name and asked her about her family. Hard to believe this was the same cowering woman Cole and his dad had practically carried into the house yesterday.

She was sweet and funny, with impeccable manners and a lilting, slow-like-honey drawl, just like Cole's. She even laughed at my lame stories about the diner, though I had to tone down Terry's pithy comebacks to a PG rating. Finally Cole let himself relax, sipping his coffee and grinning at me across the white Formica table, eyes crinkling.

"Good to see a smile on your face for a change," she said to him, stirring sugar into her second mug of coffee. "Though I suspect that's mostly your doing, Marc."

"He's got a way about him, doesn't he?" Cole replied, teasing me with his eyes. I telegraphed him a *No fucking fair!* look and pasted on a smile of my own, inwardly dreading what I needed to tell him later.

When we'd finished our coffee, Mrs. Hammond tucked her arm in mine, and I helped her hobble back out to the car on her fiberglass cast. "I'm glad to have met you, Marc," she said. "I'll admit, it's been difficult coming to terms with Cole's . . . orientation, but I can see that you two are well-suited for each other."

I smiled, genuinely touched. "Thank you, Mrs. Hammond. That means a lot."

"Call me Olivia," she replied, giving me a kiss on the cheek as Cole opened her car door.

Then he drew me aside, out of his mother's earshot. "Is it okay if I drop by tonight?"

I hesitated, swallowing hard. "I'm leaving tonight. My plane takes off at six."

Oh, Jesus. Nothing like a good kicked-in-the-teeth expression to brighten your day.

"But . . .You just got here, and now you're heading back?"

"I have to. Can't afford to take any more time off work. I spent my latest royalty check on the airfare and motel." My fingers curled tight, nails biting into my palms. "Look, I don't want to go, but there's nothing I can do here. Well, besides wait around for you to come visit, which is nice, but . . ."

"It's okay, I get it." He glanced around the parking lot before holding his hand out to me. I hated that he did that—or rather, that he felt he needed to. Even in his own home town, he couldn't be himself. "So I guess this is it?"

I wanted to throw my arms around him and kiss him goodbye, but the telltale stiffness in his back and shoulders warned me off. "I'll give you a call once I'm home. Probably won't be 'til tomorrow morning, though."

"I really, *really* wish I was going with you."

"But you're still coming back at Thanksgiving, right? That isn't so long."

He nodded and backed away. "I'd better get going. Don't want Mama to end up with heat stroke." That familiar stoic mask of his now firmly in place, he climbed into the car and drove off.

CHAPTER 24

Cole had never been great at gardening, but he was sick and tired of looking at the front lawn. It had bypassed shaggy and overgrown a couple weeks ago, and now more closely resembled a miniature jungle. His father, fiddling with the Mustang in the relative cool of the garage, gave him a half-exasperated glance as he wheeled the lawnmower down the driveway and set to work.

At barely midday, the sun was already beating down with a brutal edge. Within half an hour, Cole had soaked through his t-shirt and shorts, but he pushed on until he was done, enveloped by the familiar summery smell of gasoline and fresh-cut grass. He put the mower away, then grabbed his mother's gloves and shears and started trimming the camellia bushes. Anything to keep busy, keep his mind off Marc having left yesterday.

"Cole," came Jen's voice from the porch. How long had she been standing there? "C'mon in and have some tea with me and your mama."

He wiped his damp forehead on his sleeve. "Thanks, but I'm almost finished here. I'd rather just keep going."

"Well, I think you need a break. Your face is all red." Smiling, she placed a hand on her hip. "Don't make me come down there and drag you inside by your earlobe, because I will. Just ask my boys."

She'd actually done the same thing to him a few times back in the day. Even at seventeen, she'd had one hell of a grip. "Okay, okay, I give." He held up his hands in surrender, then charged up the stairs, dropped his tools on the porch swing, and followed her inside.

A tall, frosty glass of sweet tea was waiting for him on the kitchen table. He took a seat and gulped down a long, grateful sip. Then he got a good whiff of himself. "I should go take a shower before I stink the place up."

Jen leaned back against the counter and poured herself a glass. "We're both old married ladies. Nothing we haven't smelled before."

"Cole, we need to have a discussion," his mother interjected. She'd been in good spirits for the last couple days, sharp-witted and observant, as if the Sunday church incident had never happened. Which meant he didn't dare try to sneak anything past her. "I overheard you talking on the phone with Marc this morning. Has he already gone home? After only two days?"

Goddamn it. He knew he should've shut the bedroom door before he'd picked up Marc's call. "He had to get back to work."

"Then why didn't you go too? Aren't your classes about to start up again?"

He set his glass down slowly, steeling himself with a long breath. "I'm not going back to California for a while, Mama. You and dad need me here."

She exchanged a wide-eyed glance with Jen. "Did I hear you correctly? Did you just say you're dropping out of Berkeley for *my* sake?"

"I can apply for a leave of absence, maybe even transfer to someplace out here. There are plenty of good law schools in North Carolina."

"But isn't Berkeley supposed to be one of the best? Jen tells me if you graduate from there, you can write your own ticket."

"That's what I've heard," Jen put in.

So they'd decided to gang up on him, *Steel Magnolias*-style. Cute, but it wouldn't work. "Duke's right up there, too."

"You're already enrolled at Berkeley. You'll get delayed a

whole term, maybe even two, if you transfer to another school, and the same thing when you go back. It'll take you five years to finish a three-year degree."

"It's already decided, Mama. You're not going to change my mind."

He started to stand, but her gaze literally froze him. It was the same look he remembered from childhood—the one that said, *You'd best not mess with me, young man.*

"Cole, I don't want you to do this. Your life's in California now. Besides, what about Marc? I've never seen you so happy as you are with him. I can't let you give that up on my account."

Jesus, why couldn't she just *drop* it? He'd barely held it together the last day or so as it was. He couldn't even look at her anymore, because if he did, he'd break down completely. "I'm afraid if I go, I'll—" He stopped, swirling his glass of tea. "I just don't want to lose you."

Her hand found his across the table. "Sweetheart, you're not going to lose me. I'll live for years yet. There's all kinds of therapies my doctor wants to try. Believe me, I don't plan on leaving this world anytime soon."

Now he really did wish he'd taken a shower, because all he wanted to do was to throw his arms around her. Instead, he gave her a tight smile and nodded. "You know I could never go against you."

"That's because I'm usually right. Oh, what am I saying? I'm *always* right." She smiled back, handing Jen her glass to refill.

"Now comes the hard part," Jen said. "Talking your daddy into hiring that home health care agency."

"Is that what you want, Mama?"

"Well, I'm not crazy about the idea of strangers in our house, but I suppose I'll get used to it. All in all, it's for the best. As for your father, I'll have a little sit-down with him tonight after dinner."

Cole shook his head. "No, I'll do it. There's a couple more things he and I need to get straightened out."

As it happened, his father came looking for him instead of the other way around, glaring at Cole from the bedroom doorway as he packed his suitcase. "Your mother just told me you're leaving. Nice of you to give us sufficient notice."

"I'm flying out tomorrow, after we talk with the nice ladies from the home health care agency. They're dropping by at nine."

"'*We*'? Not damn likely. You had no right to call them without asking—"

"I had *every* right," Cole snapped. "You abdicated responsibility, so Mama and I made a command decision. This is the way she wants it. So you're going to sit down with me tomorrow and figure out how best to handle her care, and then I'm going home."

"I should've known you'd abandon us. Just like you abandoned the Corps once you decided it didn't fit in with your degenerate lifestyle."

Cole bristled, his jaw tightening. He had to count to ten to dampen the urge to tear his father a new one. "I'll call every few days, and I plan to come back at Thanksgiving. With Marc."

"If you think you're going to bring your little butt-buddy back into my house, think again."

Cole's hands fisted around the pants he was folding. "He's *my partner*, and Mama wants him to come visit."

"What about what I want?"

"Frankly, I couldn't give a fuck. I'm not rearranging my entire life just because you don't want to face reality. Mama needs you to step up, so stop behaving like a macho asshole and *do* it."

His father shoved from the doorway and marched right up into Cole's face. "I ought to give you a righteous beatdown for talking to me like that," he growled.

Cole growled right back, "Go ahead and try."

They stared each other down for what seemed like forever, until Cole figured he'd made his point and went back to packing. "I'm sure everything will be fine once you and Mama get used to the new routine. It'll be good for both of you to have someone to help with the housework and cook some decent meals. Mama didn't care for all that Chinese food you kept ordering."

"Well, she never said a damn thing to me about it."

"Or maybe you weren't listening. Just like you didn't listen when I tried to tell you the truth about me years ago."

His father snorted. "You did no such thing."

"Sure I did. The summer after my first year at the Academy—the summer I broke it off with Jen because I knew it would never work between us. You and I were sitting in the kitchen, and I was trying to explain why. But you just got up and walked out, the way you always do when you hear something you don't want to deal with."

"Why'd you need to tell me, anyway? Or tell *anybody?* Twelve years in the Corps flushed down the toilet because you couldn't shut your goddamn trap. What the hell's wrong with keeping it to yourself?"

"So it's not me being gay that bothers you as much as me *talking* about it? Well, too bad. The whole time I was growing up you kept drumming into me how important it was to develop a personal sense of honor. So how is lying honorable? Or worse, living a lie every damn day? I'm done with that. This is who I am. It's who I've always been. If you don't want to accept it, fine. But I'm not hiding anymore, from you or anyone else."

They stared each other down until his father turned and stomped away.

Terry's eyes went as big as dinner plates when I walked in the kitchen door and reached for my apron. "Jesus, you're back already? Do I want to know how it went?"

"Everything's fine, Ter. Really." I waved at Fernando, then grabbed a fresh order pad from a nearby shelf. "Cole and I have kissed and made up. Sort of."

"What's that mean?"

"Phone sex." I sighed. "Lots and *lots* of it."

Between the time difference and a fuckton of jetlag, I dragged myself through the next few hours like a marginally self-aware zombie, sorely tempted to chug coffee even though I hadn't touched the stuff in years. I plopped down in the kitchen doorway during my break and actually nodded off, until Terry's manicured nails closed over my shoulder, shaking me gently.

"Up and at 'em, buster. There's a customer out front asking to see you."

"You take care of it," I mumbled. "Won't even make you split the tip."

"Unh-uh, this one's all yours. Go on, get out there."

I'd been able to keep going as long as I'd stayed on my feet, but now it felt as if my sneakers were filled with concrete. Stumbling out front, I rubbed at bleary eyes before scanning the dining room. Closing in on seven, and only a handful of tables were occupied, all by regular customers, none of whom were trying to wave me over. So what the hell was Terry talking about?

Then I saw him—that familiar blond head and buff, gorgeous body—sitting at the same table where I'd met him that rainy Sunday afternoon last November. Stunned, I drifted over and said, "Please tell me you're not a hallucination."

"Do hallucinations get hungry? Because I could probably eat one of everything on the whole damn menu right now." With that, he got up and flung his arms around me, kissing me in front of everyone. There was some scattered applause. Terry even whistled.

I dug my fingers into Cole's jacket and held on tight. "Are you back to stay?"

He nodded.

"But how's your mom doing? Is she gonna be okay?"

"For the time being, yeah. But we can talk about it later." He kissed me again, slow, sweet and utterly devastating, like that first time in my kitchen on Thanksgiving. "Right now I just want to get some food in me and take you home."

He wolfed down the salad I brought him while Terry and I closed up, and then we headed off. When we stopped on the sidewalk in front of our apartment, Cole let out the most relieved breath I'd ever heard. "God, I've missed this place. Can't wait to stretch out in our bed."

"Well, c'mon. Paradise awaits."

Thomas met us at the door, twirling like a little black-and-white top when he saw Cole. We dragged in Cole's rolling suitcase, then he dropped to one knee to give Thomas some long-awaited pets.

I smiled. "He kept prowling the apartment crying every night while he looked for you. Just about broke my damn heart."

He scritched Thomas's ears one last time and stood, wrapping his arms around me. "Sorry I put you both through so much hell. It won't happen again, I promise."

"But you've got to go back to see your folks again sooner or later, right?"

"I told them I'd visit at Thanksgiving, with you." He flashed me a sheepish grin. "Hope that wasn't stepping over the line. I probably should've asked you first."

"What, you mean your dad's actually gonna let me through the front door?"

Cole shook his head. "Oh, you don't want to mess with my mama when she's on a mission. She can kick more ass than any drill sergeant I've ever met. By the time Thanksgiving rolls around, she'll have given my dad one hell of an attitude adjustment."

I laughed. "Well, I'll believe that when I see it." I kissed him, took him by the hand, and led him over to our bed. His jeans were looser than I remembered, sliding off his hips with barely a tug. I'd been in such a hurry to get him out of them that night in the motel, I hadn't even noticed. "You've lost weight."

He stepped back to kick them off, along with his sneakers and socks, then tugged his shirt over his head. "Guess all those household chores and yard work burned up a lot of calories." And all the stress, though I wasn't about to mention it.

Drawing close again, he skimmed a gentle hand over my hip before helping me out of my own clothes. His fingertips glided over every newly-bared inch of skin, gentle and reverent, painting shivery little tingles wherever he roamed. "God, I missed you so much. I never want us to be separated that long again."

"You won't get any arguments from me." I climbed up on the bed, pulling him along with me. He rolled onto his back and let me straddle him with no prompting at all, groaning deep as I started rubbing his shoulders. He looked even more exhausted than when I'd last seen him, fresh lines etched around his eyes. "If you'd rather go to sleep, that's fine. We can always pick up where we left off in the morning."

"Fuck sleep. Just give me a few minutes, okay? Why don't you use some of that baby oil? It usually perks me right up."

Good idea. Soon his arms, chest, and torso gleamed with warm slickness, his gorgeous cock rising against his belly, begging for my touch. But I'd only given it a few firm strokes before he gasped and knocked my hands away.

"Take it easy, or I won't last five minutes," he rasped. "Hell, before the other night, I didn't even have enough energy to jerk myself off."

"I was kind of disappointed that you never suggested phone sex."

"Jesus, I wasn't about to talk dirty to you with my parents right down the hall!"

"Aw, c'mon, it would've been fun." I grinned, leaning down for a kiss. "All exciting and secret, like making out in the back seat at Lover's Lane. Which we've never done either, come to think of it."

He chuckled. "Why don't you make a list? We'll probably get around to trying everything in the next thirty years or so."

"I like the sound of that." I dug my thumbs into his shoulder muscles, frowning at the tiny tense knots that refused to loosen no matter how hard I kneaded. When the sound of his groans shifted from pleasant to uncomfortable, I stopped. The aim here was to relax him, not hurt him. "Any special requests tonight? I'm happy to do whatever you want."

His eyes floated open, gazing hazily up at me. "Well, when I thought we were over, I really regretted never asking you to fuck me."

A hot *zing* snaked down my spine like chain lightning, a current of fresh arousal spiraling straight for my cock. "You sure?"

"Oh, yeah. Definitely." He spread his legs and tilted his hips. "I'm ready."

I remembered my first time in that Oceanside motel, the way that hot Marine had taken control, kissing and caressing me, soothing my jitters before fucking me absolutely senseless. I wanted to make Cole's first time every bit as good.

"On your stomach," I ordered, waiting for him to roll over while I squirted more oil into my hands and warmed it. His upper back muscles felt like living marble, hard and unyielding. I worked the oil into his skin and moved lower, finally reaching the small of his back. By then he'd sunk deep into the mattress, making a low, rumbling noise in his chest. Reminded me of a hibernating bear—though I had no intention of letting him fall asleep on me now.

I wiped off the oil, reached for the lube and began to open him. He gave a little start, calming a bit as I murmured, "Breathe. Relax. Enjoy." At last he gave himself permission to do just that, and my fingers breached him easily, gliding in to the last knuckle.

"Jesus, Marc, will you please *do* it? I can't stand all this teasing."

"What do you mean, teasing? This is me being all kind and considerate."

He groaned miserably, rolling over and spreading his legs again. "Whatever. Just knock it off and fuck me already."

No need to twist my arm. I got myself quickly covered and lubed, then pressed the tip of my throbbing cock to his hole. "Remember to relax, okay? And if you don't like how it feels, let me know and we'll stop. All right?"

"Yeah, okay," he huffed. "Go ahead."

I hadn't topped in a long time. Not since Rob, in fact. I wasn't prepared for all that slick, silky furnace heat. Couldn't move at first, not until Cole's moans floated to my ears.

I started out slow, giving him time to get used to all the new sensations. The times he'd fucked me had been amazing—that first deep thrust, the burn that quickly morphed into that sweet ache of being opened and filled over and over. I was nowhere near as well-hung as Cole, but when he wrapped his legs around my hips, his mouth falling open in an ecstatic moan, I felt like a damn porn star.

Didn't take long before he started thrusting back, giving as good as he got. Eyes full of fire, he pulled me down on top of him, fingers tangling in my hair, teasing my lips open with wet little flicks of his tongue.

Heat everywhere—*Cole* everywhere. Under me, surrounding me, devouring me inside and out. Too much. *Way* too much. I couldn't take any more. Grabbing his hips, I pounded him as hard as I could, hurtling toward an orgasm that grayed out the entire fucking world.

When everything finally came back into focus, I flopped onto the mattress, gulping down air. "Wow."

"No shit." Cole turned toward me, cracking open one bleary blue eye. "Christ, if I'd known your cock felt that good, I would've begged you to do this months ago."

"I told you you'd like it." As my pulse and breathing returned to normal, I leaned in for a soft kiss. "Didn't mean to go so fast your first time out, but you sure didn't act like you minded. I guess it didn't hurt, huh?"

"For about thirty seconds, then it was all pleasure." He smiled and kissed me back. "Besides, we've got plenty of time to take it slow. As in, the rest of our lives."

I let out a happy sigh. "That we do."

CHAPTER 25

December, 2010

Cole's finals ended early this term, so we drove down to spend the entire week before Christmas with my mom. It'd been ages since I'd taken more than a couple days off from the diner, so I intended to make the most of it. I sat in bed every morning with my laptop, working away on my latest project. In fact, I'd just typed "The End" and shut down the computer when Cole padded in to hand me a mug of fresh-brewed tea.

"There's something on TV you might want to see," he said.

I threw on my robe and followed him into the living room. And there was the president on Mom's thirty-two inch plasma screen, sitting at a table signing a bill with the vice president and a bunch of other politicians surrounding him. The bottom of the screen read, "President Obama signs DADT repeal into law."

"Jesus," I breathed, sinking onto the edge of the couch. "It's really happening."

"Yup." Cole reached for my hand. "And about fucking time, too."

We watched in silence until the signing ceremony ended and the president began taking questions from the press. A pretty big question swirled around in my mind. It must've been written all over my face too, because Cole just shook his head and said, "No, I'm not still thinking about going back in."

"Really?" I raised my eyebrows at him. "You didn't seem so sure last May."

"Don't get me wrong, I'm glad the bill finally passed. Now nobody else has to go through the kind of shit I did—once they implement it, anyway, which will probably take at least a year. I'll be done with law school by then, or damn close to it."

"You wouldn't have to rejoin as infantry. Even the USMC needs lawyers, right?"

"What's going on here? You trying to make me change my mind?" His smile told me he was joking.

"Look, no matter what you end up doing, I want you to be happy."

"The Corps was my home for twelve years. That's not to say I won't miss it, but I've moved on. My home's with you now." He kissed me gently. "That said, I should probably give my folks a call."

I took that as my cue to grab a shower and get dressed. I brought my laptop into the living room once I was done. The TV was still on, its sound muted while Cole talked on the phone. He said goodbye and hung up as I sat down.

"You been on there this whole time?" I asked.

"Yeah, Mama was in a chatty mood. She got to hold Jen's new baby girl at church this morning, and she just couldn't stop gushing. Apparently she's the most adorable child on the face of the planet." He gave a mock roll of his eyes.

I chuckled. "Well, her new medication sounds like it's working."

"She's probably talking Dad's ear off every damn day, though I get the feeling he doesn't mind that much," Cole replied, nodding at my laptop. "I thought you were done writing for today."

"I am. In fact, I just finished my new book, and I wanted to show it to you."

He gave me an adorably surprised little half-smile. “You never particularly cared about me reading your stuff before.”

“This one’s different.” I clicked on the file to open it, then scrolled down to the dedication, which read: *For Cole, because we lived it.* He shot me a puzzled look, which I answered by handing him the laptop. “Just read it.”

With a nod, he scrolled down to the first chapter. He’d only gotten a few pages in before he started grinning like the world’s biggest idiot. “This is about us!”

“Well, I changed the names and locations and altered a few of the more personal details, because I do eventually want to get it published. But I wrote it as a gift for you.” I leaned in to plant a kiss on his cheek. “Merry Christmas, Cole. It’s a few days early, but I didn’t figure you’d object.”

“God, Marc, thank you! This is the best present ever. But...”

“But what?”

“I didn’t get you anything.”

I laughed and threw my arms around him. “Yeah, you did.”

RP

Acknowledgments

My heartfelt thanks to Cassandra Carr, Amara Devonte, and Aleksandr Voinov for outstanding critiquing services.

Thanks also to Mari Freeman and Lori Toland for answering my pesky research questions about Raleigh and San Diego, respectively.

I owe a great debt of gratitude to the works of Steven Zeeland, specifically *The Masculine Marine* (Harrington Park Press, 1996) and *Military Trade* (Harrington Park Press, 1999), and also *Honor Bound* by Joseph Steffan (Villard Books, 1992).

Also by Cat Grant

The First Real Thing (Icon Men #1, Ellora's Cave)
Appearing Nightly (Icon Men #2, Ellora's Cave)
A Fool for You (Icon Men #3, Ellora's Cave)
Entangled Trio (Ellora's Cave)
Allegro Vivace (Amber Quill Press)
Sonata Appassionata (Amber Quill Press)

Coming Soon from Riptide Publishing:

Power Play: Resistance
Power Play: Awakening
Priceless

About the Author

Cat Grant lives by the sea in beautiful Monterey, California with one persnickety feline and entirely too many books and DVDs. In her spare time, she reads (mostly for research), goes to the movies and opera a lot and fantasizes about kinky sex with Michael Fassbender. To learn more, please visit www.catgrant.com.

CPSIA information can be obtained at www.ICGtesting.com
Printed in the USA
LVOW121217010512

279755LV00001B/13/P

9 781937 551247